A Polluted Font

The chronicles of Hugh de Singleton, surgeon

MEL STARR

The sixteenth chronicle of Hugh de Singleton, surgeon

A Polluted Font

LION FICTION

Published by
Lion Fiction
www.lionhudson.com
Part of the SPCK Group
Studio 101
The Record Hall
16–16A Baldwins Gardens
London
EC1N 7RJ

ISBN 978 1 73941 770 3
e-ISBN 978 1 73941 771 0

First edition 2023

Acknowledgments
Scripture quotations taken from the New King James Version®. Copyright © 1982 by Thomas Nelson. Used by permission. All rights reserved.

A catalogue record for this book is available from the British Library

Typeset by Fakenham Prepress Solutions, Fakenham, Norfolk.
First printed in Great Britain by Clays, Bungay, Suffolk.
eBook by Fakenham Prepress Solutions, Fakenham, Norfolk.

Another one for Susan

"An excellent wife is *the crown of her husband."*
Proverbs 12:4a

"A righteous man *who falters before the wicked*
Is like *a murky spring and a polluted well."*
Proverbs 25:26

Acknowledgments

In 2007, when he learned that I had written an as yet unpublished medieval mystery, Dr. Dan Runyon, Professor of English at Spring Arbor University, invited me to speak to his fiction-writing class about the trials of a rookie writer seeking a publisher. He sent sample chapters of Hugh de Singleton's first chronicle, *The Unquiet Bones*, to his friend Tony Collins at Lion Hudson. Thanks, Dan.

Tony has since retired and Lion has joined SPCK, but many thanks to Tony and those at Lion Hudson who saw Hugh de Singleton's potential.

Dr. John Blair of Queen's College, Oxford, has written many papers about Bampton history. These have been valuable in creating an accurate time and place for Hugh.

In the summer of 1990, Susan and I found a delightful B&B in Mavesyn Ridware, a medieval village north of Lichfield. Proprietors Tony and Lis Page became friends, and when they moved to Bampton they invited us to visit them there. Tony and Lis introduced me to Bampton and became a great source of information about the village. Tony died in 2015, only a few months after being diagnosed with cancer. He is greatly missed.

Glossary

Ambler: an easy riding horse, because it moved both right legs together, then both left legs.

Angelus: a devotional celebrated at dawn, noon, and dusk, announced by the ringing of the church bell.

Apple moise: apple sauce cooked with breadcrumbs, honey, saffron, salt, and almond milk.

Bailiff: a lord's chief manorial representative. He oversaw all operations, collected rents and fines, and enforced labor service. Not a popular fellow.

Bailiwick: the area under a bailiff's jurisdiction.

Banns: a formal announcement of intent to marry, made in the parish church for three consecutive Sundays.

Beadle: a manor official in charge of fences, hedges, enclosures, and curfew. Also called a hayward.

Bouce jane: roasted chicken, deboned and simmered in milk, pine kernels, currants, and spices.

Bruit of eggs: an egg-and-cheese custard with butter, vinegar, and either sugar or cinnamon added.

Bubo: the inflammatory swelling of a lymph gland associated with bubonic plague.

Burgher: a town merchant or tradesman.

Candlemas: February 2. This day marked the purification of Mary. Women traditionally paraded to church carrying lighted candles. Tillage of fields resumed this day.

Capon: a castrated male chicken.

Charlet of cod: fish beaten to a smooth paste, then cooked with wine, vinegar, ground almonds, sugar, and spices.

Chauces: tight-fitting trousers, often of different colors for each leg.

Childwite: a fine for having a child out of wedlock.

Churching: forty days after giving birth, a woman would meet the priest at the church porch and, accompanied by family and friends, take part in a ceremony that officially readmitted her to the church. Until that day she was ritually unclean.

Chrism: consecrated oil used in baptism and churching.

Clyster: an enema.

Cotehardie: the primary medieval outer garment. Women's were floor-length; men's ranged from mid-thigh to ankle.

Devil's door: the door in the north wall of a parish church.

Dexter: a war horse, larger than a palfrey or runcie. Also the right-hand direction.

Eeels in bruit: eels served in a sauce of white wine, breadcrumbs, onions, and spices.

Farthing: one-fourth of a penny. The smallest coin.

Fast day: Wednesday, Friday, and Saturday. Not fasting in modern terms, when no food is consumed, but days when no meat, eggs, or animal products were eaten. Fish was on the menu for those who could afford it.

Flags: flat stones used as paving.

Fraunt hemelle: an egg, meat, and breadcrumb pudding, with pepper and cloves added.

God's sibs: women who attended a lady while she was in labor, from which the word "gossip" comes.

Groat: a silver coin worth four pence.

Groom: a lower-ranking servant to a lord. Often a teenaged youth ranking above a page and below a valet.

Hall: the largest room in a castle or manor house.

Hanoney: eggs scrambled with onions, and fried.

Hens in bruit: chicken cubed and simmered in a stock of white wine, ginger, pepper, saffron, and breadcrumbs.

Lammastide: August 1, when thanks was given for a successful wheat harvest – from "loaf mass".

Let lardes: a custard of eggs, milk, pork fat, parsley, and salt.

Lierwite: a fine for sexual relations out of wedlock.

Limbo: the destination of the souls of infants who die before baptism – neither heaven nor hell.

Liripipe: a fashionably long tail attached to a man's cap and wound around the head.

Lozenges de chare: a pastry stuffed with ground pork, egg yolks, currants, chopped dates, and spices.

Lychgate: a roofed gate in the churchyard wall under which the deceased rested during the initial part of a funeral.

Marshalsea: the stables and associated accoutrements.

Martinmas: November 11. The traditional date to slaughter animals for winter food.

Maslin: bread made from a mixture of grains; commonly wheat or barley with rye.

Nice: a foolish person.

Page: a young male servant, often a youth learning the arts of chivalry before becoming a squire.

Palfrey: a riding horse with a comfortable gait.

Passing bell: the ringing of the parish church bell to indicate the death of a villager.

Pax board: an object, frequently painted with sacred scenes, that was passed through the medieval church during mass for all to kiss. Literally, "peace board".

Penny: the most common medieval coin; made of silver. Twelve pennies made a shilling and twenty shillings made a pound, although there were no shilling or pound coins.

Poll tax: a tax equal on all, rich and poor, above the age of fourteen. "Poll" from the word for head.

Porre of peas: a thick pea soup for fast days, made with onions, salt, spices, and sugar, if available.

Pottage: anything cooked in one pot, from the meanest oatmeal to a savory stew.

Pottage of whelks: whelks boiled and served in a stock of almond milk, breadcrumbs, and spices.

Rector: a priest in charge of a parish. He might be an absentee and hire a vicar or curate to serve in his place.

Rood screen: an elaborately carved wooden screen between the chancel and nave of a church.

Runcie: a common horse of a lower grade than a palfrey, often used to pull wagons and carts.

Sacristy: the room in a church where sacred vessels and vestments are stored.

St. Beornwald's Church: today the Church of St. Mary the Virgin, in the fourteenth century it was dedicated to an obscure Saxon saint said to be enshrined in the church.

St. Margaret's Day: July 20.

Sexton: a church officer who cares for church property, rings the bell, and digs graves.

Shilling: twelve pence.

Simple: honest and without guile.

Sinister: the left-hand direction.

Solar: a small private room, more easily heated than the great hall, where lords often preferred to spend time, especially in winter. Usually on an upper floor.

Sops dory: a sauce of almond milk, onions, white wine, and olive oil poured over toasted bread slices.

Squire: a young man who served as an assistant to a knight.

Stockfish: inexpensive fish, usually dried cod or haddock, consumed on fast days by those who could afford it.

Stone: fourteen pounds.

Tenant: a free peasant who rented land from a lord. He could pay his rent in labor, or, more likely by the fourteenth century, in cash.

Theriac: highly prized concoctions supposedly able to cure or alleviate most illnesses.

Toft: the land surrounding a house, often used for growing vegetables in the medieval period.

Trencher: a large platter, usually made of wood, for serving food.

Trepanier: a surgeon who specialized in removing a circular section of the skull to relieve headaches. It sometimes worked.

Tun: a large cask holding 252 gallons. The "tunnage" of a ship had nothing to do with the weight of water it displaced, but rather the number of tuns it could carry.

Verderer: an employee in charge of a lord's forests.

Vicar: a priest serving a parish but, unlike a rector, not entitled to its tithes.

Villein: a non-free peasant. He could not leave his land or service to his lord, or sell animals without permission.

But if he could escape his manor for a year and a day he would be free.

Whitsuntide: "Whitesunday" (Pentecost), seven weeks after Easter Sunday. In 1377, this was May 17.

Woad: a plant whose leaves produced a blue dye.

Dramatis personae

Hugh de Singleton	Surgeon, bailiff to Lord Gilbert, and sleuth
Lady Katherine (Kate)	Hugh de Singleton's wife
Bessie, John, and Gilbert	Hugh and Kate's children
Gilbert, Third Baron Talbot	Lord of Bampton Manor
Charles de Burgh	Lord Gilbert's nephew
Father Thomas, Father Ralph, and Father Robert	Priests at St. Beornwald's Church
Gerard, Martyn, and Piers	Clerks to the priests of St. Beornwald's
Emma Haute	Bampton's midwife
Andrew Pimm	Sexton at St. Beornwald's
Janyn Wagge	Large youth with eyes for Adela, son of Arthur Wagge (Arthur, now deceased, was Hugh's aide and companion)
Adela Parkin	Kate's servant
John Tey	Oxford locksmith
Sir Jaket Bec	Household knight to Lord Gilbert
Thomas	Sir Jaket's squire
John Faceby	Witney dyer
Harold Cooper	Witney barrel maker
John Prudhomme	Bampton Manor reeve

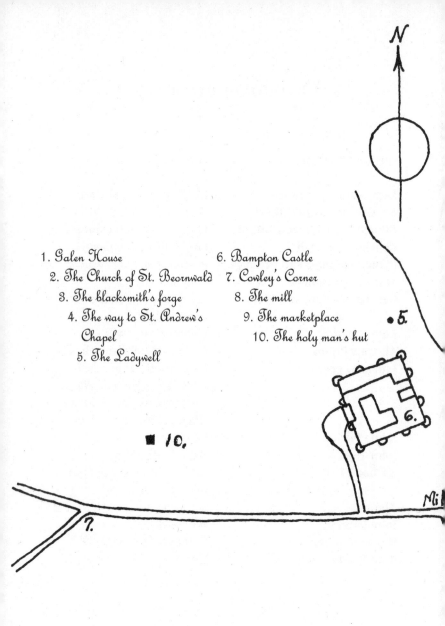

N

1. Galen House
2. The Church of St. Beornwald
3. The blacksmith's forge
4. The way to St. Andrew's Chapel
5. The Ladywell

6. Bampton Castle
7. Cowley's Corner
8. The mill
9. The marketplace
10. The holy man's hut

•5.

10.

6.

Mi

7.

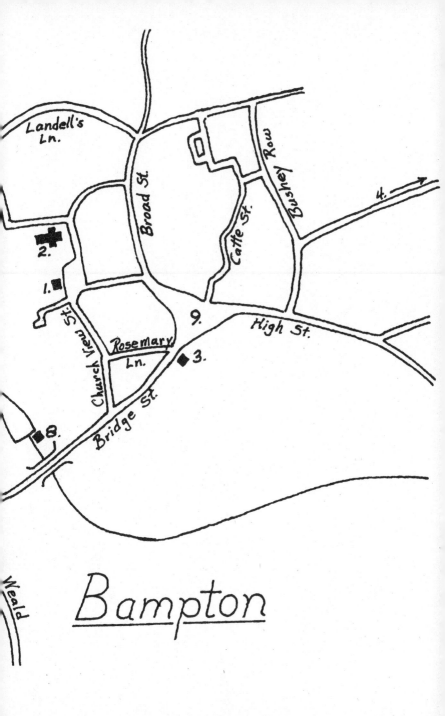

Bampton

Chapter 1

There will be no godmother, of course, for Lady Petronilla died in the summer of 1368, when plague returned. Lord Gilbert has had many opportunities to take another wife since then, but has chosen not to. However, when he volunteered to act as godfather to my new son I did not object that there would be no godmother. When a great baron of the realm makes such an offer 'twould be foolish, not to say insulting, to refuse.

I am Hugh de Singleton, a surgeon trained in Paris, and bailiff to Lord Gilbert, Third Baron Talbot, at his manor of Bampton – Sir Hugh, since Prince Edward of Woodstock granted me a knighthood five years past for services I rendered him in discovering who had slain a knight of his household.

The birth of a babe is no way man's work, even though he be a surgeon. Well, that is not always so. Many years past I was required to attend a lass when the babe she carried was wrongly presented and the midwife could not turn it. When the mother was near death, one of the god's sibs came for me. As the young woman died I opened her womb and released the child. The infant lived, and is now, if he survived the illnesses of children, ten years old. Where he may be I do not know, as his grandfather fled Bampton when he suspected I knew him to have slain the man who had set upon his maiden daughter.

Kate woke me in the night eight days after Whitsuntide and told me I must seek Emma. Emma Haute is new to Bampton, but not to midwifery. She was occupied for many years in Oxford bringing babes into the world. A widow, she removed to Bampton when she learned that the town was without a midwife since the death of Agnes Cobbe. Many midwives seek trade in Oxford. In Bampton there is no competition for her skills.

Emma is accustomed to being awakened in the night by anxious fathers. Why is it, I wonder, that babes choose to enter this life at the most inconvenient hours? At least, that is when Bessie and Sybil and John made their appearance.

When Lord Gilbert learned, many months past, that my Kate was soon to enlarge our family, he volunteered to serve as godfather. This meant, of course, that the child, were it a lad, would be named Gilbert. Kate had thought Robert, for her recently deceased father, but agreed that the benefit to the child of growing to manhood as the godson of a baron was a gift too great to discard.

If the babe were a lass I thought to name her for my mother, Maud, and Kate agreed 'twas a worthy choice. But the babe was a lad, so Maud will be held in reserve in case another babe should some day bless our household. Solomon wrote that children are like arrows, and that the man whose quiver is filled is blessed. He was silent about the wife who labored to fill the quiver.

Emma answered my thumping upon her door quickly. I believe such nocturnal banging has become so regular an occurrence that when the woman lays her head upon her pillow she is prepared to have her rest interrupted.

Emma drew a cloak over her cotehardie, then required me to enter her house and help carry the birthing stool to Church View Street. When we arrived at Galen House she announced firmly that I was to leave the premises immediately, taking Bessie and John with me. Where should I go? Wilfred, Bampton Castle's porter, would not be pleased to be awakened so early, but the sky to the northeast was already beginning to lighten and Lord Gilbert must be advised that within a few hours he would need to perform the duties of a godfather for which he had volunteered.

I hastened up the stairs of Galen House with Emma close behind. Kate was propped up in bed against her pillow and smiled when I appeared. I kissed her, told her of the midwife's requirement that I and Bessie and John be away, and then went to awaken the children.

"On your way to the castle," Emma said, "call on Joanna Huntly. Tell her to assemble some god's sibs and hasten to Galen House."

I did so, then carried John to the castle, with Bessie trailing behind. Both children rubbed their eyes, half awake but aware that the day Kate and I had told them of, when, the Lord Christ willing, they would gain a brother or sister, had finally come.

Wilfred did not answer my cries for some time when I stood at the castle moat and shouted for his attention. I feared I might awaken Lord Gilbert and all the castle residents before I heard the porter reply to my request that he lower the drawbridge and crank up the portcullis. He would have done so soon anyway, but gave evidence of displeasure when I greeted him and thanked him for his service. He tugged a forelock, but under his cap a scowl wrinkled his brow.

Many years past, when I first came to serve Lord Gilbert, he assigned me a chamber off the hall. When Kate and I wed, he gave us Galen House – the first Galen House, before Sir Simon Trillowe burned it. I took Bessie and John to the chamber, and learned it was unoccupied and contained three pallets. Lord Gilbert used the space for the servants of visiting noble guests, of which there were none at the time.

I put Bessie and John to the pallets, with instructions that they must remain until I returned. They promised, wide-eyed, to do so. And even though they were excited about the imminent arrival of a brother or sister, they seemed ready to resume their interrupted repose.

From the hall I wandered through the castle seeking John Chamberlain. Few folk were about at that hour, but for the cooks who had already begun preparations for dinner. The scent of roasting flesh caught my stomach's attention.

I found John in the kitchen, breaking his fast with a warm loaf fresh from the oven, and told him that Lord Gilbert would soon be needed. Holy Mother Church once taught, according to St. Augustine, that infants who died before baptism went to hell, corrupted by original sin as all men are. Since then, theologians have modified this view. Now 'tis thought that unbaptized babes go to limbo, a place that is neither heaven nor hell. But regardless of where the souls of unbaptized children go, I wished for Lord Gilbert to be ready to perform his duty. I asked John to seek Lord Gilbert and tell him he would soon be needed at St. Beornwald's Church. The chamberlain swallowed his last gulp of ale and departed the kitchen.

What now must I do? Join Bessie and John, and rest upon the third pallet in the guest servants' room? I knew sleep would not return. Tossing and turning upon a pallet might awaken the children. I rejected the idea.

I departed the castle to seek Father Thomas. At Shill Brook I stopped and gazed into the dark water flowing toward the Thames, London, and eventually the sea. From the corner of my eye I glimpsed movement. I saw two shadowy forms leaving Rosemary Lane, turning to the north on Church View Street. God's sibs, perhaps, on their way to share what they could of Kate's labor.

I followed. The two dark walkers did indeed halt at Galen House, rapped upon the door, and were admitted. I passed my home and saw that a candle had been lighted on the ground floor, so the women might not stumble upon the stairs, and an upper-story window also glowed dimly. No sound greeted the dawn.

Did the silence signify good, or ill?

Father Thomas should already know that his offices would soon be required. I walked past Galen House and St. Beornwald's Church to his vicarage. Neither the priest nor his new clerk, Gerard, is an early riser. Father Thomas is of advanced age, so does not rise with the dawn except when the morning Angelus devotional devolves upon him. I did not expect his clerk to be up and about either, as the glowing northeastern horizon does little to light a man's window and chase him from his bed.

Thumping upon the vicarage door did not awaken either priest or clerk quickly. But eventually I heard the bar being lifted and the clerk, rubbing his eyes, drew the door open. He likely expected bad news. A death in the town, mayhap. Certainly this was the most likely cause for him to be roused from his bed. But this day he would not be required to ring the passing bell from the tower of St. Beornwald's Church, nor walk before Father Thomas ringing a bell to tell folk that he and the priest were on a mission of Extreme Unction.

23

Gerard promised to awaken Father Thomas with the welcome news that within a few hours he would have a new parishioner to baptize. From the vicarage I was drawn back to Galen House. All was yet quiet, the windows glowing as before. I pounded upon the door and moments later Joan Colnet, a god's sib, opened.

She smiled and spoke. "Emma was about to send for you. You have a son. She wishes you to set in motion the child's baptism. When you return you may visit Lady Katherine and the babe."

Would I ever become accustomed to my Kate being "Lady Katherine" to Bampton folk?

I set off for the castle with a light heart. My Kate was well, and so, I assumed, was the babe. The rising sun had illuminated the tree tops and the spire of St. Beornwald's Church by the time I reached the castle. The drawbridge was down and the portcullis up, so I did not need to shout for Wilfred to gain entry.

The hall was quiet, the hour being much too early for grooms to prepare tables for dinner. John Chamberlain was not to be found, being apparently off on some morning duty, so I went directly to the solar to seek Lord Gilbert.

He expected me. John had advised him after my previous visit to the castle that I would soon call. A valet opened the door to the solar when I rapped upon it, and I found my employer consuming a wheaten loaf and ale to break his fast.

"All is well, then?" Lord Gilbert said when I told him of the birth of a son.

'Twas a valid question, for the arrival of a newborn is oft accompanied by trouble and sorrow rather than joy.

"Indeed. If you will attend St. Beornwald's Church at the third hour, Father Thomas will be prepared to baptize the babe."

"Hah. I will do so. With much pleasure."

From the hall I sought the guest chamber where I had deposited Bessie and John. I found them awake, rested, and ready to greet their new brother. Together we hurried to Galen House, climbed the stairs, and found the babe swaddled in fresh linen, bathed, and sleeping. Kate's eyes were also closed, but when she heard Bessie and John's excited prattle she awoke.

"He will be called Gilbert, then?" she asked softly.

"Do you object?"

"Nay. Lord Gilbert is a good man, who governs his lands well. I am content."

"As am I. The babe will be baptized at the third hour. Lord Gilbert has been notified. I will set Adela to preparing the feast. There are several fat capons in the hen house which can be set to roasting, and she can get fresh loaves from John Baker and prepare honeyed butter."

Kate smiled weakly. "You have everything well in hand," she said.

"I have by far the easiest duty," I replied.

There was yet an hour before the baptismal party was to assemble at the church porch, so I assisted Adela in catching and preparing three capons for the spit.

Most fathers absent themselves from a babe's baptism, but I am not like most fathers. I have been charged with holding unorthodox views, an accusation which is, I admit, true. I do not proclaim these opinions, for some of them, were they known to a bishop or archdeacon, could place me in peril. But observing my newborn son's baptism would not cause a bishop's eyebrows to lift, so when Emma bundled the babe and set off for the church, I followed.

Father Thomas and Gerard met us at the church porch. Lord Gilbert had not yet arrived. Great lords see no need to be punctual. They know that whatever event they are to attend will not begin without them.

We did not wait long. Lord Gilbert soon appeared, walking swiftly and accompanied by his nephew, Charles de Burgh, who serves as his page whilst learning the arts of chivalry. My employer is more accustomed to the saddle than to shoes when he must travel. His face was florid and his breathing heavy as he walked under the lychgate.

When we were assembled in the porch – Kate was, of course, not present, as her churching would not happen for forty days – Father Thomas began the ritual. He made the sign of the cross over the babe, placed salt on the child's tongue to drive out the demons which already knew of his birth and would attempt to capture his soul, then read a passage from the second chapter of St. Paul's second epistle to Timothy. The midwife had no Latin, nor had Lord Gilbert or Charles, but Gerard and I knew the words and admonition.

From the porch our party entered the church and approached the font. Martyn, Father Ralph's clerk, went to the north transept and opened the devil's door so the demons who were forbidden the soul of my son would have an escape, whilst Gerard produced a key and unlocked the lid of the font. He lifted it to set aside, and as he did so I heard Father Thomas gasp.

Chapter 2

The basin was dry. There was no holy water in which to immerse my son.

"How can this be?" Father Thomas said. Whether or not he expected an answer from those of us circling the font I cannot say. He looked to his clerk, perhaps assuming that Gerard might know.

The clerk shrugged. "The font was last employed to baptize the Hakyly babe," he said. "Richard and Philippa's lass. Father Ralph baptized the babe. The font was full then, else we would have heard."

"Indeed."

"What is to be done?" Lord Gilbert growled, no doubt considering the font dry due to some malfeasance on the part of the vicars of St. Beornwald's Church.

"Gerard," Father Thomas commanded, "hurry to the vicarage, get the bucket from the kitchen, hasten to Shill Brook and fill it, then return. Sir Hugh, will you seek Father Ralph and Father Robert, and tell them of this calamity? Ask them to hasten to the church, and together we will determine what is proper to make well what is amiss."

Gerard and I did as the vicar asked, he trotting off in one direction from the churchyard and I in another. I did not take offense at Father Thomas's charge, as a father's presence at his babe's baptism is not thought necessary by most folks. Or even desired.

I stopped first at Father Ralph's vicarage and told him of the dry font. His eyes widened in surprise and dismay, and his response was the same as Father Thomas's. "How can this be?" he said. "All was well when I baptized the Hakyly babe a fortnight past. Mayhap the font has sprung a leak. It must be inspected to learn if 'tis so. If it has, repairs must be immediately commenced. We cannot have unbaptized children facing limbo for want of holy water."

"Father Thomas would have you join him at the church straightaway," I said. "I am to seek also Father Robert and ask him to report to the church."

Father Robert is new to St. Beornwald's Church, replacing Father Harold Bokyngham. Father Harold was the nephew of the Bishop of Exeter, and during his brief tenure there was much speculation as to why a young priest with such a family connection was assigned to Bampton. I thought at the time I knew the answer to that question. My views of purgatory had somehow been brought to the bishop's ear, and Father Harold was assigned to gather evidence against me. So I thought.

But the priest made a grievous mistake when he demanded that Adela leave her service to Kate and become his housekeeper. All who heard of the requirement understood what the amorous priest wanted. When Lord Gilbert was told of this he sent a letter to Bishop Bokyngham, demanding in strong terms – I know how strong the words were, for Lord Gilbert asked me to compose the missive – that he recall his nephew to Exeter and send a replacement. Father Robert was that replacement, and from what little I knew of him seemed an amiable sort of man.

Father Robert was also shocked to learn of the dry font, as was evident in his expression when I told him.

"Father Thomas wishes me to attend him at the church?" he asked.

"Aye, he does. He, you, and Father Ralph must put your heads together and solve this calamity. Meanwhile, Gerard has gone to Shill Brook with a pail to bring back water which may be blessed, then used to baptize my son."

Gerard arrived at the church before Father Robert and I. Father Thomas had seen that one bucket of water would not fill the font, so he had sent the clerk for another. He returned moments after Father Robert and I entered the porch. The sun was now well up, the morning warming. Gerard was red-faced and breathing heavily. Running with a pail of water is not a customary activity for a scholarly clerk.

My son slept through all this tumult. He would awaken soon enough.

Father Thomas emptied the second bucket into the font, made the sign of the cross, then spoke the paternoster. Water which a few moments before had been flowing in Shill Brook was now holy water, capable of sending a soul to heaven.

Emma unwrapped my son and presented him to Father Thomas. 'Twas well this was May and a warming day. A child baptized in January would be grievously chilled. Bessie was born and baptized in November. Not so frigid a month as January, but cold enough. So far as I can tell, the plunge has done her no lasting harm.

The priest held the child over the font and asked his name.

"Gilbert," Lord Gilbert replied.

"Gilbert," Father Thomas said, "I baptize you in the name of the Father . . ." and he immersed the babe, "the Son . . . " he dipped the child into the basin a second time, "and the Holy Ghost." And into the water for the third time the child went. This last dunking brought forth a vigorous wail. As it should from a healthy infant.

Emma took the babe from Father Thomas, dried him, and dressed him in a linen christening garment, a duty which would have been that of a godmother had Lady Pertonilla not perished of plague.

Father Thomas anointed the infant's forehead with chrism, then the party moved to the altar, where Lord Gilbert made profession of faith for my son.

The ceremony now completed, 'twas time to celebrate. Our party moved from the church to Galen House. The capons were roasted, the wheaten loaves fresh, the honeyed butter prepared. All was joy and conviviality. Kate left her bed, donned a new cotehardie, and briefly joined our guests. But after consuming a bite of capon she excused herself and retired again to our chamber. Adela followed with the babe.

Charles had carried a large pouch over his shoulder all morning. When the feasting was done and the capons were nothing but skeletal remains, Lord Gilbert called the lad to himself and took the sack. From it he withdrew a large silver plate.

"For my namesake," he announced.

'Twas a valuable piece, worth near twenty shillings. Some years hence my new son will be pleased to display it upon a mantel. I hope ownership of such largess will not swell his head. Silver is a fine servant but a malignant master.

Charles is nearly a year older than Bessie. The two children seemed to enjoy each other's company whilst trying to escape John, who, being much younger, they looked upon as an unfit companion. This slight seemed not to trouble John, who kept to Bessie and Charles's heels throughout the feasting.

Gerard excused himself to go to the church and ring the bell for the noon Angelus, and Father Ralph soon followed to conduct the ritual. Others in attendance seemed to consider this a signal to depart, and as few loaves and no flesh remained there was small reason to linger. An hour after the last guest departed Galen House all trace of the festivity had been cleared away and I released Adela.

It had been a long, tiring, but joyful day. Bessie, John, and I were weary, as surely was my Kate. I mounted the steps to our chamber and found Kate and Gilbert sleeping. I descended to the ground floor and told Bessie and John to be quiet and not wake their mother. I need not have concerned myself. John curled up in a corner of the kitchen, where the ashes in the fireplace were yet warm from roasting, and was soon asleep. Bessie played with the doll her grandfather had made. All was well in Galen House.

Days are long and nights are short after Whitsuntide, so to prolong Kate's slumber I crept silently from our bed when dawn lightened our chamber window. I broke my fast with a loaf left over from the previous day, and some of the ale which remained. When Adela arrived I would need to send her to Maud Baker for an ewer of fresh ale.

At about the second hour I heard Kate stirring in our chamber and took a loaf to the stairs, where I met her descending.

"I thought to bring you this to break your fast while abed," I said.

"I am a mother," she replied, "not an invalid. I can serve myself."

"I thought only to ease your recovery," I protested.

"Which I appreciate. But I am hale, and expect to continue so."

"Not all women who give birth do so," I said.

"Indeed. And, should I suffer from ailments common to such women, I have a surgeon for a husband, who will help me recover."

If physicians, surgeons, and midwives could relieve women in distress after childbirth there would be none who perish afterward. But some do, regardless of the efforts of physicians, surgeons, and midwives. I thought it best not to mention this. A man should betimes keep some thoughts to himself.

We did not hurry to break our fast. Adela arrived with an ewer of fresh ale, and shortly after we heard a wail from the upper story. Gilbert was hungry and made this known.

A moment later I heard a knock on Galen House door. Adela ran to open it, and I heard Father Thomas ask if I was at home. I was, and offered him a cup of fresh ale, which he did not refuse.

"How may I serve you?" I asked.

"I went this morning to the font," he said. "'Twas full, as we left it yesterday after baptizing your babe."

I understood then the reason for his visit. "There is no sign of a leak?"

"None, although my eyes be not so sharp as once. Gerard could find no leak either. Perhaps you might join me and Father Ralph in seeking some reason why the font is yet full when yesterday, but a fortnight after the Hakyly babe was baptized, it had gone dry."

At the church we found Gerard gazing thoughtfully at the font.

"Days have been warm as summer approaches," Father Thomas said. "Do you suppose the holy water evaporated?"

32

"Has it done so in past summers?" I asked.

"Never. Covered as 'tis, in my memory the font has always been full and ready when needed."

"You discard and replace the holy water occasionally – is this not so?"

"Occasionally. Perhaps twice in a year. 'Tis holy water and cannot be casually disposed of."

"Indeed. But when you renew the water in the font, does the previously blessed water yet fill the basin? Or has some been lost?"

"We last renewed the holy water at Easter," Father Thomas replied. "'Twas near enough to full that I noticed no loss."

The sun was now high, so that the interior of the church was bright. I studied the font, then dropped to my knees to examine the flags upon which the font rested. I saw no hint of moisture which would tell of a leak previously undiscovered.

Gerard had earlier unlocked and removed the cover so I could inspect the basin. 'Twas of lead, hammered thin to fit the curve of the font interior. I studied the bowl and would have liked to run my hand through the water to learn if I could detect some nick or crack through which water might slowly seep. But this was holy water. I would not profane it.

Father Ralph arrived whilst we three were scratching our heads over the mysterious font. He and his clerk approached, listened to the account of the perplexing font, stroked their chins, then went about preparing for the noon Angelus.

Adela had prepared leach lombard for our dinner, and I was pleased to see Kate consume a hearty portion. Bessie could not restrain herself from jabbering about her new brother, whilst John, as is his custom, concentrated on consuming his dinner. Had he opinions about the addition to our family he kept the thoughts to himself. Kate had taught him not to speak with his mouth full. He had taken the admonition to heart, seeing therefore no reason to speak, preferring a meal to conversation.

I spent the remainder of the day about manor business. Plowing was done for the season, and planting also. Now was the time for plucking out weeds before they could smother the new crops. The men are diligent to hoe out weeds from their own strips, but not so concerned with Lord Gilbert's demesne. Unless they think that I or John Prudhomme are peering over their shoulders. Which we are.

Next morning, as I broke my fast with a maslin loaf and ale, a vigorous thumping upon Galen House door interrupted my reverie. Adela ran to answer the knocking.

'Twas Father Robert. "Father Thomas desires Sir Hugh to attend him," he said breathlessly. "It has happened again."

"What has?" I said, through the door to my hall.

"The font . . . 'tis empty."

I found Father Thomas and Gerard, Father Ralph and Martyn Raby gazing at the font, standing well away from it, as if it were a viper about to strike. The cover had been removed, and a quick glance was enough to see that Father Robert spoke true. The font was indeed dry.

"Is another baptism scheduled?" I asked. "I have not heard of another birth this day."

"Nay. The font is not needed," Father Thomas said. "'Twas but my curiosity which caused me to send Gerard here to make sure holy water yet filled the basin."

I turned to Gerard, and before I could speak he saw the question in my eyes. "The cover was in place and locked," he said. "All was in order. But when I unlocked and lifted the cover, the basin was as you see it."

I examined the flags at the base of the font and found no moisture. As there was no holy water in the basin to contaminate, I ran my fingers over the surface. I felt no crack or puncture. This did not mean there was no tiny hole through which the water might slowly drain. I grasped the edges of the basin to see if I might be able to lift it.

I was. 'Twas not fixed in place, but stayed in its position due to its weight, which was considerable even though hammered thin.

I turned the basin upside down and examined the bottom, as I had the top. I found no fissure from which the water might drain, nor was any trace of moisture found in the stones of the font which supported the basin.

Priests and clerks observed my examination silently. When I had satisfied myself that the holy water had not leaked away, I spoke to Gerard. "Where is the lock which secures the cover?"

He had set it aside on a nearby table. He retrieved it and handed it to me. 'Twas of iron; ancient, and crudely made. Likely the product of a smith more accustomed to making horseshoes and hinges than an object as complex as a lock.

"And the key?"

Gerard produced the key from his pouch. 'Twas as old as the lock; made of bronze, and worn from decades of use. I closed the lock, inserted the key, twisted it, and the lock opened easily. Mayhap too easily. I gave the key back to Gerard, snapped the lock closed, then grasped the lock and hasp, and yanked. The lock held firm. I tried the maneuver again, more forcefully. 'Twas as I suspected. The lock burst open.

Priests and clerks gazed open-mouthed at the lock.

"Useless," Father Ralph muttered.

"Aye," Father Thomas agreed. "A man could help himself to holy water whenever he wished, did he know how fragile the lock was."

"For what purpose?" Father Robert said. "A practitioner of black arts, mayhap?"

When physicians with their potions and priests with their prayers are unable to restore health, men may resort to paying those who proclaim success in black arts.

"Mayhap. Whatever the reason, we must have a new lock . . . and soon," Father Thomas said.

"Bampton's smith," I said, "might be capable of producing a lock. But it would likely be no more secure than the one I pulled open."

"To find a lock strong and well made to secure the font," Father Thomas said, "we must seek a locksmith in Oxford. There is no point in replacing an ineffective lock with another equally inadequate."

Father Robert, Father Ralph, and the clerks nodded agreement, then looked to me.

"Nay," I protested. "Kate needs me. She is a new mother."

"She has a servant to assist her," Father Thomas said.

"Adela is not a husband. And if some man has broken the lock of St. Beornwald's font and made off with holy water, the felony is not my bailiwick. 'Tis the bishop's matter, not Lord Gilbert's."

"Hah," Father Ralph said. "But the malefactor is surely of Bampton, and a tenant or villein of the manor. That would make the fellow of *your* jurisdiction."

"Mayhap. But the thief may be of the Weald, which is in the bishop's gift. And the purchase of a new lock is your business, not my own. If a man of Bampton has stolen the holy water I will not need to travel to Oxford to seek him out."

"Roads are not safe," Father Thomas protested. "A priest or clerk traveling to Oxford would be in danger."

"Send all three clerks," I countered. "There is safety in numbers."

"We are not skilled in the use of weapons," Gerard protested. "We study other matters."

"Three hale young man traveling together should be safe," I answered.

"You will not go to Oxford and seek a lock?" Father Thomas complained.

"Nay. I will seek the man who has done this theft, for surely some miscreant, probably of Bampton, has helped himself to your holy water. Evidence of a leak is absent, so some scoundrel has done this. The clerks should take the old lock and key with them to Oxford," I continued. "Mayhap a skilled locksmith can repair the lock, or use the old key in a new-made lock and thereby save the bishop a shilling or two."

I understood the clerks' reluctance to travel. King Edward, the third of that name, is aged and incompetent, and under the thumb, 'tis said, of Mistress Alice Perrers. The realm is governed badly, although since Edward of Woodstock's death his brother, John of Gaunt, is said to covet the throne. To achieve it, he would have to displace his nephew, the child Richard of Bordeaux, who is but ten years old. Joan, the lad's mother, would fight tooth and claw to see that this does not happen.

A child king! Would the coronation of a lad make the road to Oxford safer? Not likely. Folk who must travel will,

I fear, be responsible for defending themselves for years to come.

The Lord Christ taught that His followers are to love their enemies and do good to those who do them harm. Of all His teachings is there another more difficult to obey? A man who harms another and escapes the penalty due him will surely commit more felonies. A thief who robs a man upon the road will not likely consider one larceny enough and allow the next traveler to pass unmolested.

I had promised to seek the man who drained away the holy water from St. Beornwald's font. I should get about the pledge. I thought on how best to do this as I departed the churchyard.

Why would a man want holy water? To serve in the practice of black arts? To hope the application of the water would cure some disease? To sell it to another who would use it for one of these purposes?

By the time I came to Galen House 'twas time for dinner. Adela had prepared sops dory as 'twas a fast day, and I was pleased to see Kate consume an ample portion. I thought she seemed pale, which I ascribed to the modest loaf with which she broke her fast.

"What did Father Thomas want?" she asked as we ate.

I did not want to answer with Bessie present. She would absorb news of the empty font, relate the tale to her playmates, and they in turn would acquaint their parents as to the felony Bessie's father was charged to discover. The miscreant would hear of my suspicions and, being thus forewarned, attempt to hide his scheming.

"Later," I said, and cast a sideways glance to Bessie.

There came a pounding upon Galen House door as we finished our dinner. Adela scurried to answer the knock, and through the door to the hall I heard a voice ask for me. 'Twas Charles, Lord Gilbert's nephew.

"I give you good day," the lad said politely and bowed.

He is well instructed. I have been "Sir Hugh" for some years, but he will eventually outrank me. No bow will then be required.

"Lord Gilbert wishes to speak to you at the ninth hour," Charles said. "He will meet with you in the solar." As he spoke, the lad seemed to avoid meeting my eye, peering past me, seeking something. 'Twas not, I learned later, a "thing" he sought, but a person.

I thanked Charles for the message, wondered what this summons was about, and returned to Kate. When we wish to discuss matters privily I oft take a bench to the toft, where we can sit in the sun, our backs to the wall. This I did.

"A man could have no lawful reason to take water from the font," Kate said when I told her of the morning's events.

"Indeed. So to avoid a journey to Oxford to procure a new lock for the font, I have promised the vicars of St. Beornwald's that I will seek the fellow who has violated the sacred holy water."

"You believe the miscreant to be of Bampton?"

"Likely. Who else would know enough of St. Beornwald's font to know that the lock was so worn with age it could be opened with a firm wrench?"

"Why would a man of Bampton know this?"

"You have me there," I replied. "If a man stood as godfather to a newborn he would see Gerard or Piers or Martyn produce the key which would open the font lock," I continued. "A clerk would not apply force to unlock the cover. He would not need to. Indeed, priests and clerks were in attendance when I pulled the lock open with only my two hands. And I am not a burly fellow, as was Arthur."

"Or his son, Janyn," Kate said. "Have you a scheme to root out the thief?"

"I have, but I do not look forward to implementing it."

"Why not?"

"It seems to me that if a man has twice successfully drained holy water from St. Beornwald's font and not been detected, he might do so again if he has the same purpose in mind."

"So you will watch over the font?" Kate said. "Surely these thefts happened in the night. Must you forsake your bed to catch the man?"

"I intend to seek assistants. Uctred and Janyn will be willing, I think. The clerks of St. Beornwald's also. Mayhap Father Robert as well. He is young and might not miss a night's sleep once each week, as would Father Thomas and Father Ralph."

"What if the knave does not return?"

"That is a bridge I will cross when I come to it. Meanwhile, I will think on other schemes to pursue if watchfulness does not succeed."

"Word of this plan may become known," Kate said. "Folk of the castle may ask Uctred or Janyn why they abjure their beds once each week, or one of the clerks might let slip the plan to someone he trusted with the knowledge, and that man might pass the information to another less reliable."

I was prompt to meet Lord Gilbert. He pays me thirty-four shillings each year and gave me the first Galen House freehold – which dwelling Sir Simon Trillowe burned – as a gift when Kate and I wed. For these sums he does not expect to be kept waiting.

Lord Gilbert met me in the solar. He is not a man to speak in riddles nor beat around the bush. "You have, no doubt, heard rumors of the new tax that parliament has levied," he began.

I had. I had also heard that this parliament, shortly after it dissolved in early March, was being called the "Bad Parliament" for undoing some of the measures of the "Good Parliament" of the previous year – not least of which was reversing the banishment of Alice Perrers. The woman was again permitted to visit the king.

The new tax is a poll tax; one groat per person over the age of fourteen. Lord Gilbert had attended both the Good Parliament and the Bad. I awaited further remarks. Would he condemn the poll tax or approve of it? He did neither.

"I find it necessary to appoint a man to collect this tax upon my manor of Bampton," he said.

I shuddered.

"You, as my bailiff, are the logical choice."

I could not argue the logic. "Why does the king need such a sum?" I asked.

Lord Gilbert rolled his eyes. "Prince John has convinced the king that he should lead an army back to France to regain lost provinces. Hah! The king can hardly leave his bed, much less mount a horse and lead an army. But the tax is levied and must be collected. You shall do so in Bampton. Give folk until Martinmas, well after harvest, to collect the coins. But you must tell folk soon what they owe, so they may be prepared. Now, on to another matter, I have heard that the font of St. Beornwald's Church has been found dry a second time."

"Aye. 'Tis so."

"A leak?"

"Nay, no sign of that."

"What, then?"

"Some man, I fear, has taken the holy water for a malign use."

"How could he do so? The vicars keep the cover locked, do they not?"

"Aye. But the lock is old and was not well made when new. I was able to wrench it open without using the key."

"And no doubt the key is much like others, so a man could try a few keys and likely find one which would serve."

"Aye. That also."

"What will you do to uncover the miscreant?"

"I intend to set a watch in the church each night," I said. "If you agree, I will ask Janyn and Uctred to guard the font one night each week."

"You will have men to watch the other nights?"

"I believe so."

"Will one week be long enough to catch the knave?"

"Mayhap," I shrugged. "Mayhap not. I might need to continue the rota for a second week."

"Or a third," Lord Gilbert said. "Uctred and Janyn will surely agree to join the watch, and I can spare them once each week. Neither is timid about confronting a rogue."

I have been assigned work which will make for me many enemies. Because of their duty to collect rents and fines for the lord, and their reputation for avarice, most bailiffs are despised by those they oversee. My reputation is not so malign, I believe. I wrong no man for my own gain, and the folk of Bampton know this. And what town has a bailiff who can stitch the wound of an incautious laborer or set the broken arm of a lad who has tumbled from a tree whilst filching his lord's apples?

But this new task will impact my reputation badly. If not me, some other man would be assigned the duty as tax collector. All know this. Yet the onus will fall on me. Nothing I do or say will change that. When I first accepted Lord Gilbert's offer to become bailiff I understood the disagreeable duties which would occasionally fall to me. But I did not foresee collecting a poll tax. I am neither a prophet nor the son of a prophet, but I can predict my future. 'Twill not be agreeable.

Chapter 3

"**W**ho will collect the tax in the Weald?" Kate asked when I told her of the obligation Lord Gilbert had laid upon me. "Adela's father will owe twenty pence and he has barely two farthings to rub together."

"The Weald is the bishop's land. He will assign the task to the vicars of St. Beornwald's and they will likely pass it on to their clerks."

"They will collect a tax they do not have to pay? And those who cannot pay, like the Parkins, what of them?"

"The vicars collect alms for the poor of the parish. Mayhap they will devote some of the dole to help the poorest."

"You believe they would?"

"Father Thomas would be agreeable, I think. Father Ralph not so much. Father Robert is new to the parish. I cannot predict his views."

"What will become of those who cannot pay?"

"Mayhap the Sheriff of Oxford will fine those who cannot pay. Although I cannot imagine what good it will do to fine a man who has not enough coins to pay a tax. More likely a constable will be sent to seize and sell the possessions of those who do not, or cannot, pay."

"Would some men of Bampton or the Weald purchase what few goods Stephen and Emmaline Parkin own?"

"Who can know? Some would refuse, I think, even though they might profit. But a few will see a chance for gain."

"If the vicars will not aid Stephen and Emmaline, will you do so?"

"'Twould be a gift, not a loan. They would have no way to repay."

"It grieves me," Kate said softly, "to know that many folk throughout the realm will confront the same problem. 'Tis a wonder the poor do not rebel."

"The time for the collection has not yet come," I replied.

"You think there is a danger of riot and revolt?"

"If such a thing happened I would not be surprised."

"And the rebels would come first for the tax collectors," Kate said.

"As they cannot harm Prince John, whose notion the tax apparently was, they will release their anger on some closer target."

"You?"

"Aye, possibly."

From Galen House I sought Father Thomas to tell him of my scheme to watch over St. Beornwald's font in the night.

"Gerard, Martyn, and Piers will set off in the morning for Oxford," said Father Thomas. "If they are successful in finding a new lock for the font, they may return by Friday evening. With a new lock in place there will be no need to watch through the night."

"If the man who has taken the holy water learns that a new lock will be placed on the font, he may try soon what has succeeded at in the past."

"Hmm. So he might. You advise we should watch over the font until the clerks return with a new lock?"

"Aye. And mayhap the clerks will return empty-handed. It might be that an Oxford locksmith will have no suitable lock amongst his wares, and a new lock will have to be made. How long, I wonder, does it take a locksmith to make a lock?"

Father Thomas shrugged in reply. "When will you begin the night watch?" he said.

"Tonight. 'Tis unlikely the rogue will return so soon to the scene of his past felonies, but not wholly improbable. I will speak to Uctred and Janyn about watching Thursday night and Friday. Mayhap Father Robert will agree to keep vigil Saturday night if the clerks do not return by then."

"I cannot speak for Father Robert."

"I intend to seek him when I leave here, then visit the castle to invite Uctred and Janyn to participate. Lord Gilbert has already agreed to release them for their part in the scheme, and I believe they will be enthusiastic about the plan."

They were, as was Father Robert, who readily agreed to keep watch Saturday evening if no felon had been apprehended sooner and the clerks had not returned with a new lock for the font.

Days grow long and nights short. I was confident no man would enter the church for nefarious purpose until well after sunset, so after a quick supper of porre of peas I sought my bed with an injunction to Kate to wake me when darkness settled upon Church View Street.

She did. I told her to bar the door to Galen House after me and not raise it until she heard my voice next morn.

The night was as black as a pardoner's heart, the waning moon not yet risen over St. Andrew's Chapel to the east, nor due to do so for another hour or so. I entertained some worry that the man I sought might avoid Bampton's beadle and see me approach the church. I need not have concerned myself. Clouds began to gather which obscured even the stars. Had I not known where the lychgate was I might have stumbled past it.

By touch as much as sight I found the porch, pushed open the door – I must speak to Father Thomas about greasing the hinges – found my way to the font and settled myself in the corner where the base of the west and south walls meet. I ran my hand over the cover to be sure it was in place as I passed the font.

I thought I might struggle to remain awake. Not so. Sitting upon a cool stone floor with one's back pressed into a corner is not conducive to slumber.

Gerard, Martyn, and Piers got an early start. I saw them pass Rosemary Lane in the dim morning light as I departed the church and approached Galen House. I suppose I might have remained awhile longer behind the font, but to what purpose? If I could see three clerks two hundred paces distant, the miscreant I sought would know he should be seen if he approached the church . . . if anyone was from their bed so early. Would he take such a chance? I doubted he would risk his safety so.

A disagreeable task is soonest completed if soonest begun. I broke my fast with a maslin loaf and ale, then set off to notify Bampton residents of the sum due when, at Martinmas, I would return to collect the poll tax. I announced at each household that I acted for Lord Gilbert, hoping thereby to deflect opprobrium. 'Twas not my most courageous deed, I admit it. But what I told them was true.

I even sought the holy man in his hut near to Cowley's Corner. He nodded, reached into his purse, and produced four pennies. I was surprised. I had thought he would find it difficult to lay hands on four pence.

"Nay," I said. "'Tis not due 'til Martinmas."

He shrugged and placed the coins back into his purse without speaking. I've never heard him say a word.

By noon, Bampton folk knew for a certainty what had already been rumored. They knew the sum due the king by Martinmas. But though this was no surprise to many, still the news wrote dismay upon most faces.

Dinner this day was bruit of eggs, a dish I much enjoy. Most days. My appetite was this day greatly reduced, having made adversaries of most in Bampton, many of whom were former friends.

Uctred appeared at Galen House shortly before dark. I bade him wait to go to the church 'til I was sure Church View Street was shadowed enough that he would not be seen walking there. He knew where the font was located, and I told him where I had hidden in a dark corner the previous night. He tugged a forelock, peered both ways at Galen House door, then set off for the church. He had gone no more than a dozen paces when I lost sight of him in the night.

The eastern sky was aglow when I heard a thumping upon Galen House door. I expected Uctred, so had departed my bed earlier and was devouring a stale maslin loaf when he arrived. No man had entered the church, nor had he seen any man prowling about the churchyard when the first faint light of dawn illuminated the place.

"Although me eyes ain't what they was," he remarked. "Prayed at the Ladywell, but can't see no better. Me ears is good, though, an' I didn't 'ear no one about, neither."

"Was that Uctred?" Kate asked from the top of the stairs as the groom set off for the castle.

"Aye. He neither saw nor heard any man in the church."

"Who will keep watch tonight?"

"Janyn."

"What is he to do if some man enters the church and approaches the font?"

"I have told all those who watch that they are not to risk life and limb trying to apprehend the man."

"What, then?"

"They are to follow, as silently as possible, and learn where he makes his home. 'Twill not be easy on a moonless night, but the black of night can be a help as well as a hindrance. A man will be difficult to follow, but likewise he may not know he is followed."

"Janyn is robust," Kate said. "He could seize most any felon."

"Aye. Like his father, is Janyn. But if the scoundrel flashes a blade in the dark, Janyn might not see it. Nay, 'tis best to follow and observe."

Janyn, also like his father, has a principled disposition, unwilling to allow wickedness to prevail if he can do something to stop it. So when he arrived at Galen House Friday evening I made certain that he understood he was not to try to apprehend any man who might enter the church, but to follow only, as best he could. He tugged a forelock and would have set off then for the church, but I bade him tarry 'til the night became darker.

As I glanced out of the door to observe the gathering dusk I saw black-clad shapes approach. 'Twas Gerard, Martyn, and Piers, returned safe from Oxford. I bade them halt and speak of their mission, success or failure.

"The old lock might be repaired," Gerard began, "but 'twill still be weak and easily overcome. The old key is too worn to be of use in a new lock, and is of an antiquated sort that is easily and often duplicated."

"The upshot being," I said, "that the vicars must purchase a new lock. Do you have it with you?"

"Nay. 'Twill be ready next week. We are to call for it Friday."

"The cost?"

Gerard pursed his lips. "Thirty pence. Father Thomas will be dismayed. But a second locksmith we visited asked thirty-two pence."

"And told you the same thing about the old lock and key, I imagine."

"Aye, he did. Can't blame a man for desiring profit from his labor, I suppose."

"Indeed. Greet Father Thomas for me and tell him that Janyn Wagge is about to go to the church to keep vigil this night. And remind Father Robert that his watch is tomorrow night."

"If I don't catch the scoundrel tonight," Janyn said, grinning.

His words caused me to question how seriously he had taken my admonition to observe, not detain.

The four shapes vanished in the gloom; Janyn toward the church, the clerks to their various vicarages.

"Mayhap you should send two men to the church each night," Kate said. She had stood at the foot of the stairs, preparing to seek our bed, and heard the conversation with Janyn and the clerks.

"Mayhap," I agreed. "But then the watchers would need to spend every third night at St. Beornwald's, or twice as many sentries would be required. Then the chance of the villain learning of the scheme to trap him would be doubled. Twice as many opportunities for a loose tongue."

A sliver of waning moon would appear late this night. If Janyn's watch was successful, and the miscreant appeared late enough, a faint light would aid him in following. I thought that, as each night passed, the chance of the scoundrel appearing increased.

Janyn rapped upon Galen House door as dawn lightened the eastern sky. He seemed disappointed that no man had appeared, or spied and confronted him. Like his father, Janyn does not fear a tussle.

Just as the page Charles de Burgh had, Janyn peered past me into Galen House. Seeking what, I wondered? I did not speculate for long. As Janyn turned to make his way to the castle, Adela appeared in the mist of dawn where Church View Street meets Bridge Street. Janyn's face split into a sheepish grin and, had it been light enough, I believe I would have seen a blush redden his cheeks.

Shortly after the noon Angelus, Father Robert appeared at Galen House to reassure me that he remembered his part in the rota of font watchers. He promised to return at dusk and told me that before he came to Galen House he had peered under the font cover. The basin of holy water was full. No leak had depleted the supply, nor had any man evaded the watch.

As he'd promised, the priest reappeared once darkness had settled upon Church View Street. I refreshed him with a cup of ale and sent him to his assignment. He did not reappear at dawn to tell me that he had seen no man in the church, nor had I expected him to do so. Why report no report?

Chapter 4

But there was news. Gerard brought the account to me as I consumed a cup of ale. Like many others, Kate and I do not break our fast on Sunday morning. Gerard pounded upon the door and called out to me so loudly that he might have awakened folk as far away as Mill Street, were they yet abed. The shouting indicated urgency. I hurried to unbar the door and learn the cause of such clamor.

"Sir Hugh," Gerard gasped, "come quickly!"

"Where?"

"The church. 'Tis Father Robert. He lays senseless upon the floor, his head all bloody."

Kate heard this announcement from the stairs. She was correct, I thought. Two men should have watched over the font.

I trotted after Gerard to the church. On the way he breathlessly told me of the discovery of Father Robert. The clerk had gone early, along with Andrew Pimm, the sexton, to prepare for mass, and there discovered the gory sight. Andrew, he said, had remained with Father Robert, whom he had been unable to rouse from his comatose condition.

The sun was high enough that objects in the church were clearly visible, including the black-clad form lying at the rood screen and Andrew kneeling over Father Robert's motionless form.

Andrew heard and saw our approach from the porch. He stood and cried out, "Sir Hugh! You have come. He is near dead, I fear."

The sexton spoke true. Father Robert lay upon his back. Blood had clotted in his dark hair and pooled upon the flags under his head. I knelt beside the priest and touched a finger to his throat. I felt a pulse, weak but detectable, and saw his chest rise and fall. Slightly.

"Seek Father Thomas," I said to Gerard, "and Father Ralph. Father Robert is near death. One of these must be prepared to offer Extreme Unction . . . soon."

Gerard hastened away. Andrew looked on, his face gone pale, whilst I examined Father Robert. I found no other wound, only the laceration upon his pate. As gently as I could, I parted the hair and congealed blood to better see the priest's scalp. The wound was not large, no longer than my thumb, but when I probed it, the area around the gash was soft. It should not have been. A man's skull is hard unless it be fractured. Father Robert's was, I was sure of it. Some man had delivered a blow strong enough to break his head. Was this the work of a man caught removing holy water from the font? I thought this likely. What else might happen within a church to cause a man to strike down a priest?

Father Thomas, then Father Ralph, Martyn, and Piers hurried through the porch as I concluded the examination of Father Robert's skull and stood.

"Gerard told me of Father Robert's injury," Father Thomas gasped. Running is not an activity in which the rotund priest often participates. "Does he yet live?"

"Aye, he does. But mayhap not for long."

"Must he be shriven?"

This was a difficult, yet important question. If a man is given last rites but survives, he is considered as good as dead. He must fast perpetually, go bare of foot, and have no relations with his wife. This last requirement would not concern a priest, but could a vicar continue his duties if the other restraints were laid upon him?

I hesitated before answering, then finally said, "That is for you to decide."

"What is to be done?"

"He should be carried to Galen House, where I have instruments and physics to deal with this injury."

"Hurry to my vicarage," Father Thomas said to Gerard. "Get the pallet from the cook's chamber. You and Martyn can carry Father Robert to Galen House."

"Carefully," I said. "Do not jar him. I will go ahead to prepare."

As I hurried from the church I stopped at the font, lifted the lid, and glanced into the basin. It was full, the water level as high as it should be. Had Father Robert given his life to prevent the taking of holy water? Not yet. And 'twas my duty now to see that he did not.

The font was perhaps fifteen paces from where Father Robert had been found near the rood screen. Why so? Had he pursued the thief? Or sought to escape a man who had discovered him concealed near the font? If the latter, why flee toward the chancel? Flight through the porch would have been closer. Mayhap the felon was already there, obstructing an escape.

I reserve a small chamber off the hall of Galen House for treating patients. A table is there, where those afflicted with injuries may be lifted so I may spare my back when attending to the various wounds folk inflict upon themselves. Or on others. A bed is also there, where folk who must be observed may rest. If Father Robert survived the blow to his skull, he would spend much time recuperating on that bed.

I required wine, but had none. No man knows why, but wounds bathed in wine heal more readily than lacerations not so cleansed. Adela is known at the castle, so I sent her there to seek John Chamberlain and obtain an ewer of Lord Gilbert's wine. She was to inform John of what had befallen Father Robert, and tell him to make this known to Lord Gilbert. The lass did not need to be told the urgency of her charge. She gathered the skirt of her cotehardie and scurried down Church View Street.

I keep my scalpels and needles, knives and bone saws, potions and herbs, in a locked chest in our chamber. Bessie is a curious lass. I do not want her investigating such things. She shows great curiosity about my work healing men's faults. I took a selection of instruments and pouches of herbs from the chest whilst explaining to Kate what I had found in the church.

"Father Robert surprised the rogue in the act of taking holy water, you think?" she said.

"I can see no other reason why he would be attacked."

"Or why some man would be prowling about in the church at night."

"Aye, that also," I agreed.

Kate was tactful enough not to mention that she had suggested I would be wise to assign two men to watch each night. Mayhap she knew she did not need to mention this. My own thoughts would condemn me.

The bell of St. Beornwald's Church called villagers to mass as Gerard and Piers brought Father Robert to my door. Father Thomas accompanied them, whilst Father Ralph and Martyn remained at the church to conduct the mass.

Unlike my own thinning locks, Father Robert possessed the abundant curls of youth. His hair was matted with

55

dried blood, so 'twas near impossible to see clearly the nature of his injury and what must be done to promote healing. His scalp must be shaved.

Kate observed this examination from the opening between hall and kitchen.

"I need warmed water," I said, "and some of your castile soap. And also a fragment of linen or wool."

Kate left to collect these things, and a moment later Adela arrived with wine from the castle. She was not alone. Janyn accompanied her, carrying a leather ewer.

With the warmed water and soap I cleaned the dried blood from Father Robert's hair, then with a razor I shaved the area surrounding his wound. All this time he lay unmoving but for the slight rise and fall of his chest. His comatose state was a good thing. What I had next to do would surely have caused pain had he not been senseless.

I bathed the cut with wine. It has always seemed to me logical that if a wound washed in wine heals better than a laceration not so treated, the application of wine before a surgical procedure would also be wise. Most surgeons and physicians scoff at this, I know, and as the gash in Father Robert's scalp was already made, the point was moot.

Father Thomas had looked on silently. Now he spoke, asking again whether Father Robert should be shriven before I proceeded.

"Why?" I said. "He cannot answer the seven interrogations, so of what use to his soul will the sacrament be?"

"'Tis decreed by Holy Mother Church," Father Thomas said, "for the salvation of men's souls."

"You believe Father Robert's soul to be in danger? Even though he has taken vows and is a priest?"

"Uh . . . well . . . nay," Father Thomas replied. "But one must not be negligent at such a time."

"Nay, indeed. If I believe Father Robert is near to the gates of pearl I shall tell you. There will be time enough to set the host upon his tongue and recite the paternoster. As it is, he mayhap can see them not far off."

With my keenest scalpel I enlarged and laid open the laceration on Father Robert's scalp. This produced little blood. The wound had already bled copiously and the offended vessels had stopped themselves.

The crack in the priest's skull was visible. What most concerned me was a small fragment of bone which lay unattached to the skull and partially under it, driven there by the blow. A crevice in a man's skull will heal, as will any broken bone, so long as it is immobile, fixed in place for a month or so. But what of the shard which floated free? How might such a piece be held in place? My studies in Paris did not include such a topic, nor did Henri de Mandeville mention the subject in his book. I would have to resort to my own wit.

Perhaps the segment might simply be removed. Folk who suffer continual headaches often visit a trepanier, who will remove a circle of bone from the skull and release the pressure which may have caused the ache. Then the patient goes through life with a headache and also a hole in his skull, which can be no good thing, else the Lord Christ would have so designed a man's pate.

Whilst I inspected Father Robert's broken skull, others in the room backed away. I paid this no heed, but then a sudden thump captured my attention. I glanced over my shoulder and saw Piers slumped upon the floor, his eyes rolled back so only the whites were visible.

"Take him outdoors," I said, "to the fresh air. I do not need another invalid to deal with."

Gerard knelt to assist Piers, and the fallen clerk soon recovered his wits. Mostly. With Gerard's help he stood, and with wobbling steps made his way to the door.

The unattached fragment of Father Robert's skull was about the size of my thumbnail. As I studied it, a scheme took form in my mind. I had in my chest a pouch of lime. Most times when I am required to immobilize a fractured arm or leg I place sturdy reeds about the limb, then secure these with tightly wrapped linen strips or hempen cords. This method would not do for such as a man's skull. But mayhap a plaster would serve, held in place by a wrap of linen strips to form a sort of cap.

Kate was yet observing from the door, and Bessie also, peering out from behind her mother's cotehardie.

I asked Kate to go to my chest and bring from it the pouch of lime. Whilst she was about this errand I teased the bone fragment from the vicar's head and inspected what lay beneath. I found a clot of congealed blood atop a grey tissue cover to the brain. This clotted blood could serve no good purpose, so I removed it. I heard Father Thomas gasp behind me when I did so, but the priest managed to remain upright.

All this time Father Robert had remained comatose. Now his fingers began to twitch, clenching and straightening. I thought this a good sign, but if he awoke completely from his unconscious state 'twould complicate matters. I must make haste.

Kate appeared with the pouch of lime. She understood my purpose, so immediately went to the kitchen and returned with a bowl of water.

I replaced the skull fragment as near to its original place as I could, drew the scalp over the cut, then closed the wound with eight stitches. Next, I shaved Father Robert's entire scalp, so as to create a better purchase for the plaster, then washed his scalp with wine.

"I will need linen strips," I said to Kate, "to bind Father Robert's head when I have molded the plaster in place."

"Will an old kirtle suffice?"

"Aye."

Kate went to the stairs whilst I mixed lime with water and made a plaster with which to cover Father Robert's offended skull. All this time Father Thomas remained silent. Now he spoke.

"Father Robert's fingers moved a moment ago, and I thought I saw his toes quiver. Does this mean he will live?"

"I cannot say of a certainty, but I believe it a good sign. It seems to me that the longer a man so battered remains unconscious, the more likely he is to perish. But I have no evidence to confirm this."

Clenching fingers and twitching toes, good sign or not, meant I must not delay. I fashioned a ball of plaster in my hand and spread it gently over the closed wound. Surprising, is it not, how lumpy a man's skull may be? Covered with hair, these knots are invisible. Shaving made Father Robert's uneven skull obvious, but the plaster hid the protuberances and made his head smooth.

I felt warmth in the curing plaster. This was good. Should Father Robert begin to thrash about, I wanted the plaster firm and resistant to rupturing. And a layer of linen strips atop the plaster would help cushion any buffeting the priest might cause as he regained his faculties yet had not all his wits about him, that he might understand what he must not do.

Folk were walking along Church View Street, returning home from the mass, when I stood from the table upon which Father Robert lay and stretched my aching back. Most had learned of the priest's injury, and gazed curiously at Galen House as they passed. One of these, I thought, was likely the man who struck the vicar down. I have been wrong before.

Father Thomas was concerned about Father Robert, but he was also hungry, for, as with most folk, he did not break his fast this day.

"There is little reason for you to remain," I said. "I do not believe Father Robert is near death – at least, no nearer than he was three hours past – so you need not be ready to shrive him at a moment's notice. Go to your dinner. If Father Robert's condition changes, for good or ill, I will send Adela to fetch you."

Truth be told, I was eager for my own dinner. Whilst my attention was upon Father Robert's broken head, my empty stomach had not intruded upon my thoughts. But now the scent of a roasting capon wafting in from the kitchen forced hunger to the forefront.

I did not want to leave Father Robert alone whilst I ate for fear he might awaken and in his senseless state do himself some further injury. So I took a trencher to the chamber, sat upon a bench, and ate my dinner there.

I was so intent upon my meal that I did not notice when Father Robert's eyes first opened. Mayhap the scent of roasted capon jarred his senses. But when I lifted a cup of ale to my lips, my eyes fell upon the priest and I saw with a start that he gazed, unblinking, at me.

"You are awake," I said, and set aside what remained of my dinner.

Father Robert did not immediately reply, perhaps considering his answer. Then his lips moved, and I heard a whispered "aye".

"Do you know where you are or why you are here?"

Another silence followed before he said softly, "Nay."

I was concerned that the blow would so have addled his wits that Father Robert might lose any remembrance of who he was, or recognition of friends. I was relieved when he mouthed, "Sir Hugh." The words were so faint I could barely hear them, but they reassured me that, whatever miseries the priest might encounter in his recovery, amnesia would probably not be amongst them.

I called for Adela, and when she appeared told her to hasten to Father Thomas and Father Ralph with the news that Father Robert had regained his senses. I then turned back to the priest and saw that his eyes were closed. This gave me a start, but a glance at his chest disclosed that his breathing was regular. He slept, which in the circumstance was likely the best physic which could be administered. I departed the chamber quietly and finished my meal in the kitchen.

Father Thomas, Father Ralph, and the clerks arrived, breathless, and were somewhat distressed that Father Robert was not awake, alert, and able to converse. I was as well, for I had questions about his assault which only he could answer. How many men had attacked him? What weapon was used against him? Where was he when he was struck down? And, most importantly, did he recognize his assailant?

"'Tis important," I said, "that when he does awaken again someone be here to see to his needs. He will require help to use the chamber pot, and if he is lucid he must be asked what he can remember of his assault. Mayhap he

61

can name the man. The rogue will surely flee if he learns that Father Robert survived the blow and might identify him. I can attend him the remainder of this day and night. 'Twould be well if clerks could be present through the next day and night if he awakens."

This was agreed. Piers would watch Monday night, Gerard Tuesday night, and Martyn would watch over Father Robert Wednesday evening if such a vigil were yet necessary. I hoped this would not be – that Father Robert could, by Tuesday or Wednesday, carry on a dialog and deal with bodily functions, mayhap with some small assistance.

There remained from dinner a few fragments of roasted capon which, with maslin loaves, became supper for me and Kate, Bessie and John. Bessie chattered happily as we ate, as is her wont, but then suddenly fell silent and cocked her head toward the hall.

"The priest what had his head broken," she said. "He's trying to speak."

The lass's young ears had heard what Kate and I had not. 'Tis a disadvantage of age that as a man grows older and has cultivated a ripened understanding of his obligations, he begins to lose the physical prowess sometimes required to do what needs to be done. I heard nothing from the chamber wherein Father Robert lay, but trusting Bessie's ears I leapt from the bench and hurried to him.

Sunset was yet two hours off, but the chamber wherein Father Robert rested was upon the east side of Galen House, and so deeply shadowed I did not at first see the vicar's open eyes.

But he saw me, framed against an east window, and spoke. "How long have I been here?" he said softly.

"Since dawn this morning. 'Tis Sunday. You went to watch over the font Saturday evening and were struck down in the night. Do you remember?"

The priest did not immediately reply. 'Twas as if his mind required time to consider what was asked him and form an answer. I hoped this hesitation was temporary.

"Remember going to the church," he said. "Remember nothing more 'til I awoke here."

"You do not recall being attacked?"

"Nay . . . what has happened to me?"

I told the priest of his injury, although I confess I did not belabor how serious his broken head might yet prove to be. I did not want to dash his hopes of recovery.

Father Robert raised a hand to his head when I told him of the plaster and linen strips I had applied. He touched the place gingerly, and with his fingertips explored my handiwork. This investigation apparently satisfied the priest. He dropped his hand back to the blanket.

"I was watching for a man who would take holy water from the font," he said. "After that I recall nothing."

"You were found near to the rood screen. Do you remember what sent you there?"

Silence. Then, after some hesitation, the priest spoke. "I remember now. The stones behind the font were uncomfortable behind my back. I decided to sit upon the bench aside the rood screen."

"Do you recall doing so?"

"Nay."

"You remember walking to the rood screen but do not remember reaching it?"

"Aye."

"Then the man who struck you down did so as you approached the rood screen. He could have come upon you from behind if he was hiding in the porch. When you passed it he smote you with a weapon of some sort."

"I thank the Lord Christ 'twas not a blade put between my ribs. After he laid me low, did the rogue then make off with the holy water?"

"Nay. The font was full a few hours past."

"Good," the priest sighed. His eyes closed again.

I had a good supply of crushed hemp seeds to relieve his pain, also some ground willow bark and powdered lettuce sap to aid sleep, but if he did not complain of pain, nor find sleep elusive, I would save the physics for such a time as he might need them.

Lord Gilbert would want to know of Father Robert's awakening. I told Kate the priest slept and I was off to the castle but would return shortly. If Father Robert awoke whilst I was away and seemed in pain, she knew where my pouches of herbs were kept and could add some crushed hemp seeds to a cup of ale if needed.

'Twas not. I returned to Galen House well before dark and found the priest yet asleep. I did not relish the thought of sitting the night upon a bench, my back against a wall, waiting to learn if Father Robert would awaken and require aid, so I went to our chamber and carried down a supply of blankets. We had three which were oft required on cold January nights, but in summer were folded away in a chest. These I laid upon the flags and made for myself a passable bed.

Chapter 5

Morpheus did not have a firm grip on me this night. Each time Father Robert shifted in his sleep I awoke. At dawn I arose from my makeshift bed and discovered that the priest lay awake. I asked if he was hungry.

"Thirsty," he whispered.

"Do you require the chamber pot?"

"Aye."

'Twas a struggle to lift the priest to his feet. He tried to help himself and did not complain that his strength and balance betrayed him, but they clearly did. Somehow the bodily function was completed, and I got him back to his bed.

Kate heard this ordeal from above and appeared as I tucked the blanket about Father Robert. He had asked for a drink, but the effort to rise from his bed so enfeebled him that he fell immediately to sleep. For a moment I feared the activity had caused a relapse or possibly even death. Not so; his breathing was regular. Flakes of dried lettuce sap were clearly not needed.

Could the weapon used against Father Robert tell me anything of the man who had employed it? Probably not. But if I found it, mayhap it would. I broke my fast as the church bell rang for the dawn Angelus. When the observance was over, I went to the church to search for a likely cudgel.

I and the vicars and clerks of St. Beornwald's had been so concerned about Father Robert's injury that thoughts of seeking the club laid across his head had not occurred to us. I doubted it would be discovered, but if I did not search, 'twas sure it would not be.

A few years past a large silver candlestick had been used to slay a clerk of St. Beornwald's Church, so I went immediately to the altar to learn if any candlesticks were missing. Most were too small to do the damage which had caved in Father Robert's skull, but the great candlestick used against the clerk, Odo Fuller, was in its accustomed place and showed no sign of having been transformed into a weapon.

Did I seek a wooden club or an iron bar? Wood, surely. A heavy iron rod would have so crushed Father Robert's skull that no work of mine could have saved him. I prowled the church seeking a wooden stick stout enough to do the harm that had been inflicted on the vicar's head.

I found it near the churchyard wall aside the lychgate. It appeared to be a split barrel stave, useless for its intended purpose but wieldy enough to lay a man on the ground when applied to his skull. Here was likely the tool used against Father Robert. I found a trace of what seemed to be dried blood, and several hairs, caught in a crack. Whoso had laid it against Father Robert's head had hastily discarded it as he fled St. Beornwald's churchyard.

No barrel maker had resided in Bampton since plague took Henry Cooper several years past. Lord Gilbert had attempted to lure another cooper to Bampton, but the town was not large enough that a cooper would find enough custom to prosper. Even the castle would not provide enough work for a cooper to thrive. Lord Gilbert's grooms did not produce much which needed to be stored or shipped away in barrels. Rather, the castle purchased goods – wine, stockfish, and the like – which came to the castle in barrels. Barrels which could be reused.

The nearest cooper I knew of did business in Witney. Did the stave come from that town? Would a man of Witney travel to Bampton for the purpose of taking holy water from the church font? Would a man of Bampton travel to Witney to get a useless, split barrel stave with which to batter another man's skull? The former seemed more likely than the latter.

Gerard departed the church as I stood beside the churchyard wall. He gazed at me as he walked the path to the lychgate and I could see that he was curious about the object I was examining. I explained.

"Fetch Father Thomas and Father Ralph," I said. "I will remain here with the stave."

The clerk hastened away, and but a few minutes later the priests appeared. Martyn and Piers, also.

"See the stain here," I said, holding the stave before me. "And caught in the crack are some hairs which, it seems to me, match the hue of Father Robert's hair."

"Indeed," Father Ralph agreed, "although my own hair is much the same color."

"But no man has laid a club across your pate," Father Thomas said. "Where did this come from? We have no cooper in Bampton."

"The nearest is in Witney," I said. "Tomorrow I will get a palfrey from the castle marshalsea and visit the Witney cooper. Mayhap he will identify this stave as his work and be able to tell me who might have brought it here to smite Father Robert."

There was little more to say. I, the priests, and the clerks drifted toward the lychgate. Before we passed under the structure, a startling thought came to me. I stopped, turned to the church, and left the others staring at my back. The font was unlocked and would remain so until the clerks returned to Oxford and visited the locksmith who was commissioned to make a new, sturdier lock.

Mayhap Father Thomas guessed my purpose. He followed me through the porch to the font and watched as I lifted the cover. The basin was nearly dry. A few drops of holy water were in the bottom of the bowl, but the font could hold several gallons. I smote my forehead in disgust.

Father Thomas saw this act and asked, "What is the matter?"

"Look," I said, and pointed to the font.

He did. "Empty . . . again," he said.

"I was so concerned last night with Father Robert's condition that the thought of setting a watch again never occurred to me."

"Nor me," the priest said. "Who would have thought that the scoundrel would return the next night after striking down Father Robert?"

"Mayhap two men are stealing holy water. Or the thief thought the risk worth the peril if caught."

"He must believe the reward outweighs the danger," Father Thomas mused. "How could this be? Of what use is so much holy water to a man not a cleric? The man has taken ten gallons, I'd guess, mayhap more. Would he require so much for the practice of black arts?"

"If so," I said, "there is something amiss somewhere."

"Witney?"

"Perhaps – if that's where the stave came from."

"You will travel there tomorrow?"

"Aye."

Later that day I sought the castle marshalsea and requested the marshal have two palfreys ready by Tuesday at the second hour. I then found Janyn and asked if he would be willing to travel next day to Witney. He was.

When Kate learned that I intended to visit Witney on Tuesday she was adamant that I should not travel alone, and was pleased to learn that I had already secured a companion for the journey. She voiced what I had already thought – there is safety in numbers. Could this mean that the holy water thief, if he came from Witney, did not journey to Bampton alone? Or perhaps if he traveled in the night he thought a cloak of darkness would hide him.

Witney is but six miles from Bampton. Janyn and I saw no man upon the road as we traveled. Men will not journey far from home in such troubled times if 'tis not necessary to do so. We arrived in Witney well before noon and stopped at an inn to quench our thirst and enquire of the town's cooper.

We found the fellow upon Puck Lane, working his drawknife upon an oaken slat, shavings swallowing his feet to the ankles. The atmosphere was fragrant with the scent of freshly worked wood.

The cooper looked up from his work when my shadow fell across his open door. There was curiosity in his expression, for he did not recognize me as a neighbor. I had brought the near-fatal stave with me, and held it aloft as I addressed the cooper.

"I am Sir Hugh de Singleton, bailiff for Lord Gilbert, Third Baron Talbot, at his manor of Bampton." I had no reason to think that this cooper might be uncooperative, but I believed that mentioning my rank, position, and employer could do no harm.

The man tugged a forelock in response.

"Can you recognize this stave as your work?" I handed the piece to him.

He took it, turned it over in his hands, then seemed to study the bloodstain. "Don't know," he finally said. "Might be. Split when 'twas bein' shaped."

"Does that happen often?"

"Nay. If I see a board what's likely to split, I cast it aside an' don't waste me time with it."

"Have you formed staves which split before they were fully formed?"

"A few. Costs money to discard a plank without at least tryin' to make summat of it."

"What do you do with staves such as this?"

"Toss 'em out in the toft," he said, and nodded toward a closed door at the rear of his shop. "Stack 'em an' use 'em for winter fuel."

I went to the door, Janyn following, opened it, and looked into the space behind the cooper's shop and home. More than a dozen misshapen, split, or half-formed staves were piled neatly against the shop wall. A few paces beyond the staves, a narrow alley divided the property from houses upon the next street. A man who wished to take a stave from the stack would have ready access, and in the night could easily do so unseen.

But why carry a cudgel from Witney to Bampton? A man might, with little effort, find a hefty limb in the wood which bordered the road part of the way. Of course, if he walked at night he could not see in a dark forest to select a likely club. And travel at night is unsafe. Mayhap the rogue wanted a stave to protect himself along the road, and had no plan to use it in commission of his theft.

Did the weapon used against Father Robert come from

this toft? It could have. Could I prove it so? Nay. But it did not come from Bampton, so where else?

"Do folk often walk this alley?" I asked the cooper.

"Oh, aye."

"Do some take from your pile of ruined staves?"

"Aye. Folk do believe if I've cast 'em aside I've no use for 'em, an' they can help themselves."

Had this been a wasted journey? I began to believe it so. Even if I could prove the stave used against Father Robert had been drawn from the cooper's cast-offs, there was no way to identify the man who had taken it.

There was one other stop I wished to make in Witney, one other man to whom I wished to speak – the rector of St. Mary's Church. But not on an empty stomach. Janyn and I led our palfreys through the streets to an inn, and there consumed a truly deplorable dinner of let lardes made of rotten eggs, spoiled milk, and rancid bacon. Perhaps there are times when an empty stomach is preferred to a satisfied belly. The awful fare did not seem to trouble Janyn. He consumed his portion with gusto. I discover, every day I am with him, ways in which the youth is like his father. Arthur never met a meal he did not relish.

I knew where I would find the priest. The noon Angelus bell rang as we finished our meal. We stood in the churchyard, just outside the porch, until the devotional was completed and the elderly, halt, and lame had departed. Those who attend a noon devotional are usually folk too old to work and who see a meeting with St. Peter in their near future. They hope by regular attendance at the Angelus to gain favor with the Lord Christ and thereby ensure His approval.

The priest followed his flock through the porch. I introduced myself and Janyn.

"Heard of you," he replied. "Father Thomas speaks well of you. A surgeon, I understand, as well as a bailiff. What brings you to Witney? Are you upon Lord Gilbert's business?"

"In a way. Has any holy water gone missing from your font?"

The question seemed to baffle the priest. "Why do you ask?" he said.

"Because the font at St. Beornwald's Church has been emptied several times in the past fortnight, and 'tis sure some scoundrel has done it, for the font has been carefully examined for leaks."

"And there are none?"

"None."

"Is the font not locked?"

"It was, but the lock was old and easily forced. A new lock is being made, but until 'tis ready we thought to set a watch over the font."

"Were you successful in protecting it?"

"Nay. The new priest at Bampton, Father Robert, was set upon Saturday night and was found Sunday morning with his skull broken."

"Dead?"

"Nay. I patched his broken head and I believe he will live. The weapon used against him was a malformed barrel stave, likely made here in Witney, as we have no cooper in Bampton."

"You have spoken to Harold Cooper?"

"Aye. Whether or not the stave came from his shop he cannot say. Regarding your font, is it secure? Has any holy water gone missing?"

"Your words cause me worry. Follow me. We will inspect the font."

A few moments later I stood before an elaborately carved font furnished with an equally intricate cover. This was fastened to the base with an iron hinge on one side and a sturdy hasp and lock upon the other.

"Wait here," the priest said. "The key is in the sacristy."

A few moments later the rector reappeared with the key. I knew what we would find before he applied key to lock and raised the lid. The basin was full. Stealing holy water from this font would be a nearly impossible challenge. If a man of Witney wanted a convenient source of holy water he would not find it here.

A priest knows much about the lives of folk within his parish, but if St. Mary's rector knew something by way of the confessional, he would not speak to me of it. Nevertheless, I asked.

"Are there rumors about Witney of any man – or woman – practicing black arts and using holy water in performing the apostacy?"

The rector seemed to take the question as an affront. His back stiffened and his brow furrowed. "Nay," he said firmly. "Folk of this parish are guided properly."

"But surely some, even with the best instruction, go astray. Consider Judas, who spent three years with the Lord Christ, yet betrayed Him."

The priest was silent for a moment. "Aye, I grant you that," he finally admitted. "I will keep my ears open and send you word if I learn of any sorcery or divination in Witney."

I bade the rector good day, and Janyn and I mounted our palfreys and set off for Bampton.

"Think you the holy water thief is from Witney?" Janyn asked.

"Mayhap, although what he might do with so much holy water I cannot guess."

"Could a man sell holy water?" Janyn asked.

"If he could find a customer. The question of what a buyer would do with so much holy water leads us back to heresy and black arts."

"Is there no beneficial use for holy water? Babes are baptized in it. It must do some good, eh?"

"Well, aye. But that is only when a priest directs its use."

"Mayhap there's a priest somewhere what needs holy water," Janyn suggested.

"He could pray over his font and make his own," I said.

"Oh . . . aye."

We rode silently for the last few miles to Bampton.

Father Thomas decided not to replace the holy water until the new lock was ready. To do so would mean again setting a rota to watch over the font, and experience told us that such vigilance might not be successful. I agreed with the priest. I did not want to practice my surgical skills on another broken head.

By Wednesday, Father Robert was able to rise unaided from his pallet, although he was unsteady when he did so, and complained of a headache and occasionally saw two of what was but one object. I gave him crushed hemp seeds in a cup of ale twice each day. Mayhap the physic relieved his discomfort. I kept him at Galen House so I could be at his side if he suffered a relapse. Once Piers had been to Oxford and returned with the new lock, and could look after his priest's recovery, this would be soon enough for Father Robert to return to his vicarage.

The three clerks departed Bampton early Friday morning. I saw their shadows pass the windows of Galen House at the first hour. 'Tis fifteen miles to Oxford. A long walk, especially for men who generally journeyed no farther than from vicarage to church in a day's travel. They are young, but I knew that by the time they returned on Saturday they would be footsore.

They were indeed. And empty-handed. They had, they told me, just approached Swinford upon their return when two men, armed with daggers, burst from the forested verge, seized the lock, and vanished into the wood. The thieves took nothing else. Of course, clerks would not likely possess anything much worth stealing – not whilst upon the road – but these knaves seemed to know of the new lock. Martyn had carried it, he said, in a way that was visible to the villains. But once they had seized the lock they sought nothing else.

Had these scoundrels followed the clerks from Oxford, knowing what they carried? Had the thieves wished to be certain that the font in St. Beornwald's Church remained unsecured? I asked the clerks if they had recognized their attackers. They had not. They would have known men of Bampton or the Weald.

Father Thomas was furious for two reasons: the lost thirty pence and his yet unprotected font. "Next time, *you* must go to Oxford for a lock," Father Thomas growled at me. "And take that strapping lad and two daggers with you."

I had assured Father Thomas that three clerks could travel safely to Oxford and return, so in a manner of speaking it was my fault the new lock had been stolen.

"I'll do better than that," I said. "I'll take Sir Jaket also."

"He's one of Lord Gilbert's household knights, is he not?"

"Indeed. And he wields a sword with authority."

"When will you go?"

"Monday. Mounted, we should be able to travel to Oxford and return in one day."

"The beasts will not appreciate the journey."

"True. Especially the palfrey Janyn rides."

The font at St. Beornwald's Church would remain dry. This could not be helped. To my knowledge, no wife of Bampton was near to giving birth. Mayhap a wife in the Weald was pregnant. I do not know well the folk who reside there, as 'tis not my bailiwick. But if necessary, more water could be hauled to the church and blessed. Of course, the holy water would have to be discarded in a proper manner after the baptismal to prevent it being stolen and misused again. That was a bridge we would cross only if and when we came to it.

The locksmith from whom the clerks had purchased the stolen lock had his shop on St. Mildred's Street, near to Northgate Street. On Monday the fellow listened as I explained the need for a lock such as the one he had provided for three clerks a few days past. He did not seem much surprised that the lock had been stolen. I thought this odd. He was an aged fellow. Mayhap in his many years he had seen much evil, so that new transgressions no longer astonished him. Locks are to prevent theft, not to be the cause of it.

"Has any man tried to sell you the lock since it was taken last Friday?" I asked.

"Nay, and had any man done so I'd know 'twas my work."

"How so?"

"I engrave my initials on the case: 'JT'."

"Do other locksmiths of Oxford do the same?"

"There's but one other locksmith. He leaves his work unmarked."

"If we return Friday, will you have a duplicate lock ready? For thirty shillings?"

"Aye."

"Who is the other Oxford locksmith?"

"Thomas Pyke. You'll not get from him a better price than I offer."

"Where is his shop? I wish to alert him of the stolen lock, so if any man tries to sell it to him he will know its history."

"Oh, aye, an' he'll see me letters stamped on it. Thomas's shop be on High Street, near to St. Mary the Virgin."

We bade the locksmith good day. 'Twas time for dinner, so before I sought the other locksmith we repaired to the Fox and Hounds and devoured a roasted capon. I believe Janyn could have consumed the fat fowl himself. When we finished the meal he looked upon the pile of bones with something akin to remorse.

The locksmith we next visited had not been offered a new lock. He knew of the manner in which John Tey marked his work. This was why, he said, a thief would not likely try to dispose of purloined goods in Oxford.

By the time we splashed across the Thames at Swinford our mounts were fatigued. I considered stopping for the night at Eynsham Abbey, where I knew we would be welcome. But the thought of leaving my Kate and our babes alone for the night caused me to press on.

The days grew long, so we reached Bampton before dark. The palfreys were exhausted, and Sir Jaket, Janyn, and I were saddle sore, but we had accomplished our mission. I did not, however, look forward to repeating the journey come Friday. I left Janyn and Sir Jaket at Church View Street and walked to Galen House, whilst my companions took themselves and my palfrey to the castle.

My Kate greeted me warmly, as I expected she would, and this was another reason not to linger at Eynsham. A pea and bean pottage simmered upon the hearth, and while we ate our supper I told her of the day's events.

"If the locksmith desired more custom," Kate said when I concluded the account, "he might send men to accost the clerks upon the road and bring the lock back to him in Oxford. He could then sell it to you Friday and gain thirty more pence." My Kate is a wary woman, perhaps because she is wed to a bailiff. "The locksmith would have to pay a few pence to the felons who stole from the clerks and seized the lock. Yet his profit would be great."

"It would. And when I return to Oxford Friday and fetch the new lock, there will be no way to know if it is the same lock the clerks were given."

"Perhaps the locksmith is an honest man," Kate said. "We may be seeing malfeasance where none is."

"We? It was you who broached the idea that the locksmith might be dishonest."

"You would have thought of it on your own." Kate smiled sweetly. "Now, I hear Gilbert calling for his supper."

Bessie and John had been privy to this conversation, and when her mother had departed, Bessie spoke. "You must return to Oxford Friday?" she asked.

"Aye."

"With Janyn and Sir Jaket?"

"Aye."

"What if men with daggers and swords set upon you as you return?"

"Three armed men will be safe."

"Not if they are attacked by six armed men."

The lass had a point. But would an unscrupulous locksmith hire six men to retrieve a twice-sold lock?

Could he? The cost would severely dilute his ill-gotten profit. Mayhap collecting another man to travel with us to Oxford would be wise. Uctred is a castle groom who has in the past been useful when muscle was needed to subdue villains. I would ask him the next day. And Thomas, Sir Jaket's squire, would add another dagger to our armory.

Was it my imagination or did the folk of Bampton now wear sullen expressions when their gaze fell upon me? If this was not an illusion, I was sure of the reason for their scowls. I had told them a few days past what they owed the king. The poll tax weighed heavy upon them.

So when on Tuesday and Wednesday and Thursday I walked the town with John Prudhomme to observe flocks and the weeding of Lord Gilbert's demesne lands, many folk turned their backs to me. They would not do so to John. It was I who had earned their disgust.

Uctred was pleased to escape the drudgery of the castle for a day, even if it meant he would return in the evening tender in the nether regions. Uctred is not young, and his eyes are weak, but if a man is close enough to use a dagger against him, Uctred is capable of taking care of himself. He had been at Poitiers with Lord Gilbert's father.

Chapter 6

$f$our palfreys and Sir Jaket's ambler were ready in the marshalsea Friday morning at dawn. The ambler set a swift pace, which the palfreys could match only at a gallop. Sir Jaket grinned at our discomfort, but slowed his mount to spare us. We reined our beasts to a halt before the locksmith's shop at the third hour. I could purchase the lock, consume a brief fast-day dinner, and be home by the ninth hour. So I thought.

The locksmith's shutters were down. He was not yet open for business. This surprised me. A burgher seeking custom should certainly welcome patrons by the third hour. Mayhap the man was ill. Rumors had come to Bampton that plague had returned to Oxford, although the sickness seemed less virulent than in past outbreaks. So men said.

I dismounted and rapped firmly upon the door. There was no response. And oddly enough, a sturdy lock was fixed to a hasp to secure the door. If the locksmith was within, why not simply bar the door? A lock would be necessary only if he was away. He could not twist a key in a lock on the exterior of his door if he was within. Or could he?

An alley behind the shop gave access to the rear of establishments which fronted onto St. Mildred's Street. I went there and thumped heartily upon the rear door, then called out when I received no response. An upper-story window was open the width of my hand, so if the locksmith were abed with a fever or some other malady he would, were he alive, hear me call his name. Yet no response.

No lock secured the rear door. None was required if the locksmith departed his shop through the front door. Why would he do so? He knew I was to call this day and pay him thirty pence for another lock. Mayhap he had forgotten the appointment. The lock secured to the front door was evidence he was not within, unless he had locked the front door, walked to the alley, entered his shop from the rear, then barred the rear door from inside his shop.

I and my companions sought an early dinner at the Fox and Hounds, then returned to St. Mildred's Street. Mayhap, I thought, if the locksmith had simply forgotten our appointment he would shortly return.

We consumed eels in bruit and barley loaves for our dinner, then returned to St. Mildred's Street. The shutters were yet down and the lock still fastened the door. Of John Tey there was no sign. Was the fellow prosperous enough that he could overlook thirty pence?

Was there any reason to linger in Oxford, awaiting, hoping, for the locksmith's return? Mayhap he had been called away from the town and would not return for many days. Sir Jaket, Thomas, Janyn, Uctred and I discussed our options and decided that none were good, but the best was to return to Bampton, then return to Oxford some day next week.

As I mounted my palfrey and gazed one last time at the locked door and closed shutters, a speck of white shoved under one of the shutters caught my eye. It seemed to be a fragment of parchment or paper. I dismounted, and while my companions looked on, wondering what I was about, I went to the shutter and pulled out a scrap of parchment from under the boards.

"What have you found?" Sir Jaket asked.

"A message," I replied.

"To the locksmith?"

"So it seems."

"What does it say?"

"'He came. I will pay tomorrow.'"

"That's all?"

"Aye."

"Who is 'he'?" Janyn asked.

"Me, I suspect. The message was not here when we first sought the locksmith. Some man tucked it under the shutter while we were at our dinner."

"Has some other man purchased the lock made for St. Beornwald's Church?" Sir Jaket said. "Mayhap the locksmith is absent because he has been offered a better price for our lock. He is away so he does not need to keep his bargain."

"What is to be done?" Uctred said. "Must you seek the other locksmith?"

"Nay. This locksmith is obligated to keep his promise. If he does not, I will seek the sheriff. Sir Roger is a friend to Lord Gilbert and I've had dealings with him in the past. He'll fine the locksmith should he not keep his part in the bargain."

"This means another journey to Oxford," Uctred said.

"Perhaps not. Janyn and I will remain in Oxford 'til tomorrow. Sir Jaket, you, Uctred, and Thomas return to Bampton. Two armed men should be safe upon the road. Tell Lady Katherine I am delayed in Oxford and will return tomorrow. Explain also to Father Thomas this complication. Janyn and I will seek lodgings for the night at the castle. Sir Roger will have an empty chamber or two. In the morning I will confront John Tey and take possession of the promised lock."

"That he has perhaps promised to another," Sir Jaket growled.

"So it seems. Why else would some fellow promise to pay for something tomorrow? What else would a locksmith have to sell?"

Janyn and I led our beasts to the castle and turned them over to the marshalsea. A serjeant greeted us and took a message to the sheriff that two of Lord Gilbert's men requested lodgings for the night.

When these arrangements were completed, we set off for the other locksmith. If for some reason I could not have a lock from John Tey, I might secure another. Not so. Thomas Pyke claimed the press of business forbade him from promising another lock. Not for a month or more.

My head had just dented the pillow when, in reviewing the day's unrewarding events, the parchment fragment I had taken from under the shutter came to mind. John Tey would not read it, for it was folded in my pouch. Whoso wrote it expected the fellow to return to his shop, find it, and be ready Saturday to receive payment for something. Was the locksmith expected to return this day, or in the night? Did he know to seek a message under a shutter? Would he open his shop tomorrow, or would he assume something was amiss when he found no message and stay away? 'Twas past curfew. I admonished myself for not considering that Tey might have expected a message and would guess that whatever plot he was involved in had gone awry.

Next morning Janyn and I broke our fast with maslin loaves and ale, then hurried to St. Mildred's Street and the locksmith's shop. I did not expect the place to be open for business and it was not.

On one side of John Tey's shop a glover did business; on the other a signboard proclaimed an herbalist resided within who could cure most ills. Both of these establishments were open for custom. I entered the glover's business first.

The proprietor coiled his hands together and smiled unctuously. The smile faded when I asked if he knew the whereabouts of John Tey and he realized I intended no purchase – although his merchandise seemed of good quality and I might have been persuaded to buy.

"John? Nay, I've not seen 'im these two days now."

"Has he a wife? Or family residing in Oxford?"

"Wife perished of the pestilence. Had a son what studied at Magdalen College."

"Did the lad graduate?"

"Aye. Think so."

"Does he live nearby?"

"Don't know."

"Does John speak of him?"

"Nay. Quiet, like, is John."

"Does Tey complain of business being bad?"

"Never 'eard 'im do so. Always seems to 'ave trade. Some man banged upon 'is door and called for 'im yesterday. Customer, I s'pose."

"Likely," I agreed.

Janyn and I departed the glover's shop and entered the apothecary's establishment. The fellow sat before a wall of flasks and containers of sweet-smelling herbs. I was familiar with the labels affixed to most of these. Indeed, I use some of them, especially those which may reduce pain.

The herbalist's replies were much like those of the glover. He did not know where the locksmith had gone. He did not know where the son now resided. He did not know when Tey might return. And nay, Tey had not complained of a lack of custom.

I had used crushed hemp seeds to help soothe Father Robert's painful head, so decided to purchase a pouch to renew my store. When might I return to Oxford to resupply my chest of herbs? Not soon, I hoped. But that might depend upon a fugitive locksmith.

As the herbalist measured out a sack of hemp seeds, I noticed behind the apothecary a small barrel capable of holding perhaps seven or eight gallons, hardly larger than a flask. I wondered what palliative was stored therein. A liquid, no doubt, and not likely a curative useful to a surgeon. More likely a clyster or some such remedy useful more to a physician than a surgeon. I do not sniff men's urine and tell them to change their diet from warm foods to cool, or from dry to moist. Their bile is of no interest to me, nor their humors. When I set a man's broken arm I know that, if he follows my counsel, the bone will mend. If a physician's advice is followed, however, there is often no improvement in the patient's complaint. If consuming prescribed foods could cure diseases, who would die if they did as their leech instructed?

The herbalist saw me idly gazing at the small barrel. He then did a strange thing. As he handed me the hemp seeds, he sidled to his dexter side, so that his corpulent form obscured my view of the vessel. I paid no heed to this. I should have.

As Janyn and I departed the apothecary shop a richly garbed man entered. He recognized, by the cut and quality of my cotehardie, that I was his equal, and bowed slightly as we met. A physician, perhaps, come to the herbalist to renew his supply of physics.

John Tey could not be found, and the locksmith I could find had protested that the press of business made it impossible for him to manufacture a new lock for many weeks. I did not believe him. Nevertheless, I went to the High Street to speak again to the fellow who had declined my business. His response this day was the same as last. He must decline my business until the backlog of work was reduced.

Why do men do some things and refuse to do others? Mayhap they are guided by convictions. What part could a man's beliefs play in his decision whether or not he should make a lock for the font of St. Beornwald's Church? More than likely profit motivated such a choice. Could the locksmiths of Oxford earn more coin by refusing to sell a lock than by doing so? Who would pay them, and why?

To return to the castle we walked on St. Mildred's Street past the glover, locksmith, and apothecary. The glover and apothecary were entertaining customers, but John Tey's shutters were yet down. As we passed these establishments a man departed the apothecary shop. The fellow was garbed in a green cotehardie of finest wool and wore a cap of darker green, complete with a long liripipe. This customer was younger than the man who had entered the place as Janyn and I departed. Younger than me, I think, for his closely trimmed beard showed no sign of silvery whiskers. He carried in his hand a stoppered leather flask, looked both ways upon St. Mildred's Street, then hurried away, ignoring Janyn and me.

A young physician collecting physics to treat a patient, I thought. What would he carry away in a leather flask? Most medicines are dry, powdered, or ground fine, then mixed with ale or wine for consumption. Mayhap the flask contained some physic already mixed and ready for use.

A clyster, perhaps, from the small barrel in the herbalist's shop.

There was no reason to linger in Oxford. As we made our way through the teeming streets to the castle marshalsea, I heard a passing bell ring from St. Michael's at the Northgate. The pestilence? Men and women die every day, for many reasons, but plague has slain so many since it first entered the realm that the sound of a passing bell drives my thoughts to the pernicious malady.

I dwelt upon such morbid thoughts as Janyn and I mounted our palfreys at the marshalsea, crossed Bookbinders' Bridge, passed Osney Abbey, and set off for Bampton. My mission was a failure.

Nay. Not completely. I was not returning to Bampton with a lock, but I was returning with information. Someone did not want the font of St. Beornwald's Church to be secure. And they were willing to pay to see that it was not.

Who could profit so well from this that they would be ready to pay to keep matters as they were? Could folk who practiced black arts find such a ritual profitable?

"Penny for your thoughts," Janyn said as we approached Swinford. Lost in consideration of locks and barrel staves and battered priests, I made a poor traveling companion.

I reviewed our discoveries, or lack of discoveries, of the past hours. Janyn had, of course, heard my questions and the responses.

"Mayhap you ain't never goin' to discover who stole the holy water an' struck down Father Robert."

"Mayhap. But I am not yet ready to admit failure. Last week I read a passage from the book of Proverbs, in my Bible, which bears upon this riddle: 'A righteous *man* who falters before the wicked *Is like* a murky spring and a polluted well.'"

"You ain't goin' to give way to the wicked?"

"Not yet. If I can discover who smote Father Robert, I'll know who took St. Beornwald's holy water. Or mayhap the discovery will be the other way round."

"Find him what took the holy water an' you'll know who hit Father Robert, eh?"

"Just so."

"An' them Oxford locksmiths is mixed up in the business, you think?"

"Aye. Somehow. But what a reluctant locksmith would have to do with an attack upon a priest I can only guess."

"Me father said when riddles like this came, you'd soon figure it out."

"Not always soon," I said.

I dismounted where Church View Street joined Bridge Street and walked home, while Janyn took my palfrey to the castle marshalsea. I was late for dinner at Galen House, but as it was a fast day I did not miss much – a pottage of peas and beans flavored with onions, and a maslin loaf with no butter. The meal did nothing to improve my melancholy, but Bessie's cheerful prattle did.

I had a beauteous and amiable wife, three healthy babes, and a comfortable home. Should my inability to find a felon obscure these blessings? 'Tis all too easy to think on what is lost rather than what is gained. I must learn to take all things as they come, and be content.

I did not linger over my pottage – who would? – but set off for Father Robert's vicarage to learn how he fared. Piers answered my rapping at the vicarage door, and before I could ask, provided a report of the priest's condition.

"Sir Hugh, you are well met. I was about to call at Galen House."

"Is Father Robert unwell?" I asked.

"Nay. 'Tis otherwise I intended to report. Come and see."

The clerk led me to the vicarage kitchen, where I found Father Robert spooning pottage into his mouth. He looked up to see his caller and his face split into a wide grin. As well it might. He was alive and enjoying nourishment – well, as much, I suppose, as a man can enjoy an oat and barley pottage – when he might, had matters evolved differently, be occupying a corner of St. Beornwald's churchyard.

When he saw me enter the vicarage kitchen, Father Robert rose from his bench in greeting. To do so he placed his hands upon the table to steady himself. It was evident that without some support he might totter and fall.

"Sir Hugh," the priest greeted me. "As you can see, I am mending."

"I am pleased," I replied. "But I perceive yet some weakness, so I beg you to be seated and finish your meal. Since we last spoke, do you remember any more of the night you were attacked?"

"I think of little else, but no matter how long I review that night, nothing more comes to mind."

"The man knew you were assigned to watch over the font," I said. "Or, if not you, that some other man had been so appointed. Else he would not have entered the church armed with a cudgel."

"Did he propose to slay me, do you think, or but cause me to be insensible?"

"He did not smite you a second time. What this might mean I cannot guess. Mayhap he believed one blow would serve his purpose."

"But then he fled," Father Robert said, "and his purpose was forgotten."

"Aye. Even though you lay insensible upon the flags, he did not take time to withdraw holy water from the font, but took to his heels – in such a hurry that he discarded the weapon he used against you."

"The barrel stave?"

"Aye. He surely brought it believing he might need a way to do violence against anyone who attempted to subvert his scheme. Why else possess it?"

Father Robert was silent for a time, then spoke. "I did not enjoy the blow to my skull, nor do I rejoice in the headache I now endure, but the fellow might have slid a dagger betwixt my ribs. I wonder why he did not."

"Mayhap he does not own one," I said.

"What? Too poor to own a dagger?"

"I begin to think so. And a dagger cannot be used to render a man insensible. Its use means death. There is no half way with a blade. It is possible that a man pierced will live, but the man using the dagger does not intend that his victim should survive."

"So the man who attacked me did not intend my death, you think?"

"I do not say so. He may have intended to slay you with the only weapon he possessed."

"Then why run before he was sure I was dead?"

"Who can know?" I shrugged. "When I find the man, I will ask. Now, regarding your convalescence, a moment ago you spoke of a headache. Does the ache come and go, or is it with you always?"

"Comes and goes. Mostly comes."

"While in Oxford I renewed my supply of hemp seeds. Send Piers to Galen House this evening and I will give him a pouch. Mix a thimble-full of crushed seeds in a cup of ale twice each day, morning and evening, or thrice, if the discomfort is great.

"When you stand," I continued, "do you walk unaided, or must Piers or a servant assist you?"

"I require aid," the priest sighed. "My left leg is weak and collapses under me."

"What of your left arm and hand?"

"They are also feeble."

"Can you move the arm?"

"Aye. But it will not obey my commands. I tried this day to lift a cup of ale to my lips, but had no strength and the cup fell from my fingers."

I had seen a similar result some years past when Lord Gilbert's verderer was slow in moving from under a tree his sons were felling, and a branch caught him across his head. Ever after he walked with a limp, and the sinister side of his body was impaired. Why this should be so I do not know, as the falling tree smote the dexter side of his head. Henri de Mondeville did not address this in *Surgery*. Mayhap the same affliction would not come to Father Robert. I decided not to tell him of the verderer. There would be time enough for bad news if good news was not forthcoming.

Father Thomas and Father Ralph needed to be told of the strange circumstance of locksmiths who declined custom. When I departed Father Robert's vicarage I went first to Father Thomas. He is senior of the vicars who serve St. Beornwald's Church, and has been assigned to Bampton since before my arrival in the town fourteen years past.

To hold a conversation with Father Thomas it is necessary to speak clearly and with raised voice. The priest has suffered the disease of the ears for as long as I have known him, and this affliction has no cure. Indeed, it becomes worse as the years pass.

Gerard opened to my knock, invited me to sit upon a bench in the modest hall, then set off to seek the priest. He might have called for him, but 'twas unlikely Father Thomas would hear anything less than a shout, and a yell to announce a visitor would be undignified.

The priest expected me to have a new lock and key, I believe. Sir Jaket, he said, had called Friday to tell him I was delayed in my mission but would attend him Saturday. He had mentioned nothing, Father Thomas said, about a failure to procure the new lock.

So when I explained my failure, the priest's eyes widened in astonishment. Who would expect a burgher to turn down trade?

"What can be the reason for this?" Father Thomas said when I concluded the tale.

"I have an opinion," I said.

"I would hear it."

"Men go into trade to make a profit. No burgher seeks to reduce the weight of his purse."

"What is your point?"

"The locksmiths of Oxford can earn more coin by not making a lock for the Church of St. Beornwald than by doing so."

"How can this be? Is some man paying them to abjure our business?"

"So I believe. Stealing holy water from St. Beornwald's font has been profitable. Whoever has done so wants to continue, which he may not be able to do if the church has a new lock."

"Profitable enough that he could bribe two locksmiths? Astonishing."

"Indeed. I would not have thought that the practice of black arts could be so lucrative."

"You believe that is why the font has been emptied so many times?"

"Why else? And it is so gainful that some man risked the noose when he smote Father Robert."

"If he is practicing black arts, he risks a noose whether he assails a priest or not."

"I called upon Father Robert this morning," Father Thomas said, "after the dawn Angelus. You have surely saved his life. He seems likely to be good as new when his skull knits . . . What? You think not?" Father Thomas must have seen in my solemn expression that I was not as sanguine as he. "Is something amiss?" he continued.

"Do you remember Lord Gilbert's verderer, who a decade past got in the way of a falling tree and was struck upon the dexter side of his head?"

"Aye – much like Father Robert's injury."

"Indeed. Ever after he favored his left arm and leg. Walked with a limp and his left hand was weak."

"The same may befall Father Robert?"

"It may."

Father Thomas crossed himself. "I will pray that it does not."

"I have done all I know to do," I replied. "Any more is indeed work for the Lord Christ."

Chapter 7

Bampton, Witney, Oxford. How were the events and men of these places tied together? Or were they not? Mayhap I saw connections where none were. But I did not believe so. If the three places were linked, it was most likely by one man. Perhaps two. But no more. The more who are involved in a felony, the more likely one will let slip an incriminating word or do some suspicious deed which will lead to the unraveling of the plot. Even felons know this, so limit their companions in malicious behavior to no more than necessary to achieve their malign ends. And the fewer felons, the fewer to share the profits of their villainy.

"Will *you* tell Father Ralph this vexing news," Father Thomas said, "or shall I?"

"You may do so. Lord Gilbert will want to know of the dilemma in which his manor church is caught. If I go to the castle now, I can see him before he takes his supper."

Lord Gilbert was in his solar, entertaining Sir Nicholas Mainwaring and his lady. I was uncertain whether or not I should tell all of what I had learned, but he absolved me of the decision.

"Sir Jaket reported that the locksmith who was to make a new lock for St. Beornwald's font is not to be found," he said.

"Indeed."

"Can you not purchase a lock from some other locksmith? Surely more than one man follows that trade in Oxford."

"One other. But he protests that the press of business makes him unable to devise a lock for a month or more."

"Hah! During which time the font will be open to all with a ladle and bucket – unless you mount a guard. Although when last you did, the result was disagreeable."

"No man will take holy water from the font," I said.

"Oh? Why so?" Lord Gilbert replied, raising one eyebrow, as he is wont to do when he is skeptical of an answer.

"'Tis dry, and will not be filled again until we have a lock or it is needed for a baptism."

"If no lock is ready but a baptism is required, what then?"

"That is a bridge to be crossed when we come to it. No woman of Bampton is near to giving birth, so mayhap the matter will be resolved before the next babe arrives."

"Mayhap. On another matter, Sir Nicholas has brought word from Richmond. The king has taken to his bed at Sheen Palace and is not expected to rise from it."

"The realm will have a child king," I said.

"Aye. Richard of Bordeaux is but ten years old."

"Who will be regent?"

"Who indeed? There will be numerous volunteers for the post. His mother, and his uncle John foremost."

"The news causes the want of a lock to pale in comparison," I said. "Will a parliament be called?"

"I pray not. The last caused enough harm to continue for some years."

"The poll tax?"

"Indeed. Prince John desires to make a name for himself as a great warrior, like Richard's father. To do so he needs to lead men in victorious battle. Soldiers must be paid. Wars cost money."

"A new parliament would call for more taxes?" I asked.

"Hah! When did a king ever summon parliament for a purpose other than raising money?"

Here was a question even a dolt could answer. Never.

A bell rang in the castle hall. A valet was calling Lord Gilbert, his guests, and the servants to their supper. This did not include me. I bade my employer good day, and set out for Galen House.

At Shill Brook I stopped on the bridge to watch the flow. What difference was there between the water of this stream and the water of a font? Aye, one has been blessed by a priest, but what special properties did that give it? The Lord Christ was baptized in a river. No priest spoke a blessing over the Jordan, and no bishop ordained John the Baptist. Were these heretical thoughts? I have been accused of unorthodox opinions. I will share these thoughts with no man. But my Kate will understand.

Father Robert appeared at mass Sunday morning, but only with Piers's support. I saw the priest and clerk approach as I and Bessie and John passed under the lychgate. Kate, of course, remained at Galen House with Gilbert. Her lying-in would not end 'til her churching, some three weeks hence.

Father Robert tottered unsteadily and dragged his left foot, but he wore a determined expression. If the priest was so tenacious that he would worship the Lord Christ but two weeks after being so grievously wounded, should I not be equally resolved to discover his assailant?

Piers guided Father Robert to a bench and the priest collapsed with a sigh. I took the bench immediately behind him and observed his movements. I did not like what I saw. He would lean to his sinister side, then suddenly jerk himself upright. A few moments later he would repeat the process.

Father Ralph spoke the homily. He is not the most animated speaker. I saw several men, and a woman also, tilt to one side or another, then lurch back to vertical. But these did not have the excuse of a broken skull.

Father Thomas passed the pax board to conclude the mass. I waited just outside the porch with my impatient children for Father Robert and Piers to appear. They had waited until all others departed the sanctuary. Mayhap the priest feared he would stumble against some parishioner. Or that some unsteady parishioner would stumble against him.

Bessie and John were eager to go home. They knew that Adela and their mother had prepared fraunt hemelle for our dinner, and Adela was even now hurrying from the church to Galen House to finish preparing the pudding.

They would have to wait. I wished to follow and observe Father Robert as he and Piers made their way to his vicarage. I suppose I might have sent Bessie on home with John. 'Tis little more than two hundred paces from St. Beornwald's Church to Galen House. Likely Bessie would accuse me of being too protective. I plead guilty.

The journey from church to vicarage was slow. Piers retarded his pace to match Father Robert's. I thought the priest dragged his foot more than when, an hour earlier, he had approached the church. Priest and clerk knew I followed, and surely knew why. I worried that the priest might aggravate his fragile condition by exerting himself overmuch.

When the two men reached the vicarage door, Father Robert turned to me and grinned through his discomfort. "I made it," he said. But no sooner had the words left his lips than his leg buckled under him and he dropped to the threshold.

Piers and I helped the priest to regain his feet. Fortunately, he had fallen away from the door, else he might have struck his head against the jamb and cracked open the protective plaster with which I had covered his head.

Piers and I supported the priest and took him to his bed. This we accomplished with no help from Father Robert's sinister leg, which he dragged uselessly. His left arm also seemed of little benefit. Piers braced Father Robert and flushed with the effort. Likely the priest had not broken his fast this Sunday morning. I thought his weakness might partly be due to hunger as well as his affliction, so as soon as we stretched the priest upon his bed, I sought the vicarage kitchen and the cook.

The scent of hens in bruit caused my empty stomach to growl. The cook glanced up from his simmering pot, surprised to see me rather than Piers. He stood, a question in his expression.

I replied. "Father Robert is abed. The effort to attend mass this morning was, I fear, too much in his weakened state. He is too unsteady to eat his dinner at a table. You or Piers must take a bowl and spoon to him and see that he consumes an ample meal."

Piers had followed me to the kitchen after we'd settled Father Robert upon his bed. I turned to him. "After Father Robert has consumed his dinner, he must rest. I can think of no reason he might want to leave his bed, but if he does you must tell him I forbid it. Only to use the chamber pot may he rise. Sleep and rest are his greatest needs."

"I will see that he has both," the clerk said.

Bessie and John had peered through the vicarage door whilst Father Robert was put to bed and I gave instructions to the cook and clerk. No doubt they had also smelled the hens in bruit and their stomachs had reacted much like my own. I gathered them up and we trotted off to Galen House and our own dinner.

'Twas difficult to be content with fraunt hemelle after inhaling the scent of hens in bruit. Normally I would be well content with fraunt hemelle for my dinner. Most folk are satisfied with their lot until they see another whose possessions are greater. Which, if true, means there are few contented folk in England.

While we ate, I told Kate of Father Robert's collapse.

"He should have stayed abed and not attended mass, then?" she said.

"Aye. Although what he did is common enough. Injured folk who are freshly rested do not understand that any small exertion will weaken them."

"This happened to Father Robert?"

"So I believe. And he had not broken his fast."

"Most folk do not of a Sunday," Kate replied.

"Aye. But neither are they recovering from a broken skull."

I woke early on Monday morn. Kate's rooster can be relied upon to greet the dawn. Likely he believes the sun rises to hear him crow.

It seemed to me that the answer to the disappearance of St. Beornwald's holy water lay in Witney, as that was probably the source of the splintered stave which cracked Father Robert's skull. I resolved to travel there again. Not alone. I am no coward, but neither am I nice. I would seek the castle and require Janyn to accompany me. He would be pleased to escape castle drudgery. But first I would visit Father Robert. His relapse troubled me.

In the night, a scheme to discover if any man yet sought holy water from St. Beornwald's now-empty font had come to me. The lid of the font was of carved oak, darkened with age. And the font was located in a dark corner of the church. A small stone positioned upon the lid would be displaced if a man lifted the lid to learn if the holy water had been replaced. Did the folk of Bampton know that the font had been left dry to prevent any more thefts? Some surely did. There had been no attempt to keep the news secret. Would a man of Witney know this? Not unless he came to Bampton in the night and found the font dry.

I found Father Robert at his table, in violation of my instructions. Piers saw my frown and raised his palms upward in a sign of exasperation. The priest had heard my admonition a few hours earlier and evidently thought an explanation was in order.

"Ah, Sir Hugh. I am well recovered," he said.

"Until the next time you attempt too much activity."

"Worship of the Lord Christ is never too much effort."

"So you will leave, then, tomorrow to make pilgrimage to Canterbury and worship at Becket's shrine?"

Silence followed.

Sarcasm was lost on Father Robert, as when he finally spoke, he said softly, "I have long desired to do so, but even next week will be too soon, would you not agree? Many times in my life I have prayed to the saint, that he might make straight my path. Perhaps his intercession is why I am alive today."

"Mayhap," I muttered. Indeed, I am not so boastful that when a patient recovers I claim my competence the sole reason for the fellow's mending. Father Robert's convalescence had progressed beyond my expectation. Was this St. Thomas's work, interceding with the Lord Christ for Father Robert? 'Tis well to think the Lord Christ's work my own at times.

"You may be stronger now than yesterday," I said, "but you are not yet strong. You must rest. That will be your best treatment this day forward."

"For how long must I remain an invalid?"

"Until St. Margaret's Day. Even after that you must go carefully."

"I will do so," the priest sighed.

From the vicarage I walked to St. Beornwald's Church to carry out my scheme. In the path between the lychgate and porch I found a small, flat pebble about the size of my thumbnail. This I placed in a carved groove on the font lid. Then I lifted the lid to be sure the stone would slide off if the lid were raised. It did. I replaced the stone and set off for the castle.

Janyn was pleased to escape the mundane labors of a castle groom yet again. I told him to have two palfreys ready after dinner and we would travel to Witney.

My dinner this day was lozenges de chare, which was surely a more pleasing repast than Janyn would enjoy. Although he did not speak of his meal as we traveled, Lord Gilbert is becoming parsimonious due to many debts, and I doubt his grooms' dinner was elaborate.

We reached Witney shortly after noon, and I called upon the rector of St. Mary's Church. The noon Angelus had just been concluded and I found the priest in the church porch, where the elderly of his flock greeted him as they passed. Most who attend the noon Angelus are near the gates of pearl and hope to ensure their passage through that portal by acts of piety.

The priest was more cooperative than when we first met. After considering Judas, he no longer seemed to think that if some of his flock were practicing black arts their doing so reflected badly upon him.

I asked the rector if his font was filled with holy water.

"It was four days past," he said, "when I baptized a babe."

"You have not examined it since then?"

"Nay. The lock is strong and the key is hid in the vestry."

"Do your clerks know where 'tis hid?"

"Aye. But they are honest fellows. They would not ladle holy water from the font for use in the black arts."

"You are sure of this?"

"Aye. But I will get the key and you will see."

The rector left us at the font and hurried away, his robe flapping about his bony ankles. The key must have been in an easily accessible place, for he reappeared as quickly as it takes to write of it.

As the priest had said, both lock and key were nearly new. He fitted the key to the lock, twisted it, opened the lock, and when it was free lifted the lid. The font was nearly dry. Only a trace of water remained in the base of the bowl.

The priest gazed wide-eyed into the font, then stepped back as if he'd seen a viper coiled in its depths. He was struck dumb for a moment.

"What has happened?" he said, as if he thought I would know.

I did. At least, I thought I knew why the font was nearly dry. How it became so was another matter.

"The font in St. Beornwald's Church has been left dry for many days," I said, "to prevent some scoundrel making off with the holy water for some nefarious purpose. As he cannot obtain a supply in Bampton, he has come here."

"But the key—"

"You said your clerks know where it is hidden. Do any others? When you went to the sacristy to retrieve it, you were not gone long."

"So far as I know, only my clerks know of its location."

"What of the sexton?"

"Oh, aye. He might know."

"Show me where it was concealed."

The plan of St. Mary's Church was much like that of St. Beornwald's. The sacristy was off the chancel, a small, narrow chamber no more than three paces wide and six paces long. A rack was fastened to one wall, upon which the priest's surplice was hung. Beside that was a chest.

The rector went to the chest, lifted the lid, and pointed to a slot in the lid. "Here is where the key is kept," he said, and to illustrate he slid the key into its housing, then closed the lid.

"The chest is not locked?" I said.

"Nay. Why do so? No man enters, but for me and the clerks and the sexton. And only vestments and parish records and such are within."

"Folk who are to wed come here to sign the banns, do they not? And as no church is locked in the night, anyone might enter here and seek the key."

"How would they know where to look?" the priest said.

I glanced about the room. A table was drawn against the end wall, and there was a bench nearby. The chest filled with parish records, and the rack for the rector's robes and surplice, were the only other objects in the chamber.

"Where else would a man seek a key? How many men of Witney know the font is locked, and that you produce the key after visiting the sacristy? Dozens, I'd wager."

"More like hundreds," the priest admitted, "but the windows are narrow. How could a man scour the sacristy on a dark night? He could not see what he sought."

"How many candles burn through the night in the south aisle?" I asked.

"Those are lighted by folk who wish to pray the souls of parents and other folk from purgatory. To use them for some profane purpose would be sacrilege."

"Indeed. But would a man willing to steal holy water care about another sacrilegious act?"

The priest was silent, considering the thought. "Probably not," he finally said.

"You must find another place for the key to the font lid, else you may expect to lose more holy water."

The priest looked about the sacristy, seeking some secure location.

"Not here," I said. "If the thief does not find the key in the chest, he will seek it some other place in the sacristy, and there are few places he would need to search."

The rector considered my suggestion, gazed at the key, then brightened. "I will hide it in the rectory, where even my clerks will not know its location. Even men practicing black arts will not ransack my lodging."

From the church, Jányn and I sought Harold Cooper. If a man stole holy water from a church font he would need a container in which to carry off his booty. No large barrel would serve; such a vessel would weigh ten stone or more.

Even a small barrel. If a man carried away holy water, his cask would need to be small. Unless, of course, two men were involved. This was possible, but I had my doubts. A man might carry away holy water in a bucket, I supposed, but why avail himself of a barrel stave when seeking holy water in Bampton?

Janyn and I led the palfreys to Puck Lane and the cooper's shop. We found him fitting staves to a barrel base. He was not pleased, I think, to be drawn from this delicate work. If the staves are not precisely fitted to the base the finished barrel will leak.

The barrel under construction was large, probably half a tun. Filled, it would be rolled to its destination, or carried to a wagon by a brace of stout men.

I watched as the cooper fitted an iron band about the base of the gathered staves. When he had completed the task to his satisfaction he looked up, stretched, and spoke.

"You be the bailiff from Bampton?"

"Aye."

"You seekin' cast-off staves?"

"Nay. I seek another thing. Do you make small barrels?"

"Make 'em whatever size a man might want. What size you need?"

"Not for myself. Have you recently made a small barrel for some man?"

"How recent, an' how small?"

"Large enough to store five or six gallons, no more, so that a man could carry it unaided. And made within the past three or four months."

"Hmm. Made a barrel 'bout that size a year past, think it was. Folk don't often want a barrel that size. Cost near as much as a larger one an' takes as long to make."

The cooper had made a small, easily transported barrel a year ago, but the theft of holy water from St. Beornwald's font had begun but a month past. So I believed. At least, that's when the loss was discovered.

Would a small barrel be purchased for some other use, then when its purpose ended, be pressed into use for holy water devoted to the black arts? Who could know?

Janyn and I returned to Bampton whilst the sun was yet well above the forest to the west. I dismounted before Galen House, sent Janyn to the castle with the palfreys, and went to my supper – a porre of peas flavored with a few bits of pork. I was well content. With the meal. Not with what I had learned this day.

Kate noticed, and asked the reason for my solemnity. I told her of the holy water missing from St. Mary's Church and the cooper's assertion that he had not made a small barrel for a year.

"If a man wished to carry away holy water, he could do it in a leather ewer," Kate said. "He'd not need a barrel."

"Indeed, even a hollowed wooden tankard would serve. But few ewers or tankards could contain all the holy water in a font."

"You think the thief from Witney?" Kate asked.

"Perhaps. If he's from Bampton he will know the vicars are leaving the font dry so holy water cannot be used for some corrupt purpose."

"Will he?" Kate said.

"Probably. Gossip travels fast."

"And if he is from Witney he may have visited St. Beornwald's font in the night, found it dry, and decided to seek holy water nearer to home."

"He will be unable to do so in the future," I said. "The rector of St. Mary's Church plans to hide the key to his font lid in his rectory, in a place even his clerks will not know."

"Is the lock new and strong?"

"Aye. He will not need to seek a better."

"But you will?"

"Aye. Else the font in St. Beornwald's Church will remain dry."

"Until Gwinith Watkins is delivered of her babe," Kate said.

"When is that to be?"

"Lammastide," she said. "So the vicars will not need to replace the holy water for a month or more."

"And by that time I may know if the thief is from Bampton or some other town."

"How so?"

I explained to Kate what I had done with the small pebble.

"Ah," she exclaimed. "If the stone has fallen away, then 'tis likely the rogue will be of some other place."

"Just so. If the holy water is replaced, folk in Bampton will know. If it is not, they will know that also. Folk will pass the word. If the thief is of Witney, he will no longer be able to renew his supply of holy water from St. Mary's, as the key to the font lock is now safely hidden."

"So he may visit St. Beornwald's Church to see if there be holy water in the font."

"And when he lifts the lid, the stone will be displaced. Evidence that the man is of Witney, or Burford, or Eynsham."

"Or some other place," Kate concluded. "But not likely Bampton . . . Unless the font lid being lifted is a coincidence, having nothing to do with either missing or replaced holy water. But I've heard you say bailiffs do not believe in coincidences."

"What of bailiffs' wives?"

"Them also," Kate smiled. "Now, I hear Gilbert demanding his supper."

Chapter 8

How long would it take for some man of Witney to realize he could no longer procure holy water from the St. Mary's Church font? A day? Two days? A week? Would he then seek holy water in Burford? Most churches have fonts secured with locks sturdier than the one which had served St. Beornwald's Church. The only reason holy water was taken from St. Mary's Church was that the key was readily available. Would this be so in Burford or Eynsham? Or did the priests of those towns exercise greater caution than the rector of Witney, concealing the keys to their font locks more carefully?

I was impatient. Next morning, after breaking my fast with half a maslin loaf and ale, I hurried to St. Beornwald's Church. Father Ralph and Martyn were leaving the porch, having just concluded the dawn Angelus, when I passed under the lychgate. I greeted them, but then hurried past. They probably wondered what brought me to the church so early, but I was not about to tell them. Three may keep a secret if two are dead.

Fewer worshipers attend the dawn Angelus than the noon or dusk observances. In the summer, when days are long, folk object to leaving their beds so early to begin the day, and in winter, days are short but mornings are cold, and a warm bed is a stronger attraction than ritual.

The church was vacant when I passed through the porch to the nave. No one saw me go to the font and inspect the lid. No one saw as I found the pebble where I had left it. No one had lifted the lid to inspect the basin.

I was disappointed. Did this mean the holy water thief knew the font was dry? Or did it mean he had not yet discovered he could obtain no more holy water from St. Mary's Church? If the former, the man was likely of Bampton. If the latter, he might be from anywhere.

Mayhap I should visit John Tey again. Unannounced. The man's shop was closed three days past. Surely it would no longer be. How could a man make a living if he shuttered his shop to customers?

I went to the castle, found Sir Jaket, Thomas, and Janyn, and requested they accompany me to Oxford on the morrow. This they were quite willing to do. Life in a castle can become tedious, although most villeins, tenants, and cotters would be willing to exchange domiciles.

Returning from the castle I called on Father Robert to learn how he fared and tell him that I was bound for Oxford on the morrow, so would not visit him again until Thursday. The priest seemed hale enough, considering his injury. But his left arm hung limply from his shoulder, and when he adjusted his position on the bench he did so using his dexter leg only.

Muscles become stronger with use. I must consider some exercise I could prescribe which might restore Father Robert's weakened arm and leg. It would be something to puzzle about on Wednesday as I rode to Oxford.

Rain overnight had turned the roads to mud. Our palfreys and Sir Jaket's ambler were muddied past the fetlocks by the time we passed Osney Abbey. I did not stop at the Fox and Hounds to stable our beasts, but went directly to St. Mildred's Street. The locksmith's shutters were raised. He had returned and was open for business.

Thomas and Janyn held our beasts whilst Sir Jaket and I entered the shop. Tey looked up from his bench and smiled. He had seen me before but had perhaps forgotten, and now thought I was a well-heeled customer seeking a lock to secure his considerable possessions.

I disabused him of the notion and refreshed his memory. "Two weeks past you sold a lock to three clerks of St. Beornwald's Church. As they took it home they were set upon near to Swinford and the lock was stolen. I came here a few days after, seeking another lock, and you told me to return in four days and you would have another lock ready for me. But when I did, your shutters were down and you were not to be found. I see now on your bench a lock being assembled. Who is it for?"

"Uh . . . Roger Greene."

I noticed that Tey had hesitated before providing a name. "Where does the man reside? Is he a burgher of Oxford? Mayhap for a few pence he will allow this lock you have nearly completed to go to Bampton and be willing to await another."

"Uh . . . mayhap."

"Is the fellow prosperous? What is his trade?"

"Cobbler."

"Nearby?"

"Aye. Shop on Blue Boar Street."

"We will visit him and learn if he will consign this lock to St. Beornwald's Church in exchange for, let us say, six pence."

"No need. I'm sure Roger would consent. Leave the six pence with me. I'll see he receives it when I tell him he'll have to wait a fortnight for his lock."

Was there a cobbler on Blue Boar Street who would delay taking possession of a lock for six pence? I suspected not. I believed that John Tey had been caught out and saw no way clear but to sell me the lock he had been paid to withhold and reap an extra six pence into the bargain.

"Is this lock nearly complete?" I asked.

"Aye. I must file a rough edge or two."

"It will be ready tomorrow?"

"Aye."

"We will call for it at the second hour. Be here and have it ready. Sir Jaket and I and our men will seek lodgings at the castle, as Sheriff de Elmerugg is a great friend of Lord Gilbert. Sir Roger will be unhappy if I return here tomorrow and find you gone." Whether or not he would, I could not say, but 'twould be well if Tey thought so.

The locksmith bowed as we departed the shop. I believe he was convinced.

We took the long way to Oxford Castle, walking the length of Blue Boar Street. No cobbler did business there. I could save Father Thomas six pence with this knowledge.

After a night at the castle – which was delightfully free of vermin, unlike the Fox and Hounds, where lodgers awaken infested with fleas and lice – we headed for the locksmith's.

Mentioning Sir Roger and Lord Gilbert the day before had had a salutary effect. John Tey was present in his shop at the second hour, the lock and key resting upon a table before him.

"I give you good day," I said, then reached into my pouch and fished out four groats and sixteen pennies.

"And six pence for the cobbler whose lock this was to be," Tey said.

"I sought him yesterday and gave him the six pence," I lied. The locksmith knew this to be a falsehood, but what could he do? His lie was caught out by another.

I placed lock and key in my saddlebag, and we four set out for Bampton. I was pleased that the business of stolen holy water from Bampton's font was at an end. Whoso wanted holy water for heretical use would have to seek it from some other place.

But there was yet the attack on Father Robert to probe. Finding the attacker would surely end any threat to St. Beornwald's font, even if a new lock had already done so.

Splashing across the Thames at Swinford can be a chilling experience, but not in June. The day was warm and the cool water was agreeable. My chauces were wet to my thighs, but dried before we passed the gate to Eynsham Abbey.

I dismounted where Church View Street joins Bridge Street, withdrew the new lock and key from the saddlebag, and walked north to Galen House, whilst Sir Jaket, Thomas, and Janyn made for the castle with the beasts. They would be late for their dinner. As was I.

Kate was pleased that I had finally procured a new lock for St. Beornwald's font. I was pleased that my dinner was nearly ready. Kate had held back from frying hanoney until my return, so the dish was ready but a short time after I opened the door.

After dinner I called on Father Thomas. Procuring the new lock had been trouble enough. I wished the thing to be some other man's responsibility. The priest was delighted to see the new lock, and would not be content until we had hastened to the church and fitted the lock to the lid.

Father Thomas was as gleeful as a child with a new toy. He inserted the key and opened the lock, then snapped it closed and opened it again. Several times.

"We shall have no more stolen holy water," he said. "I will see Father Ralph this day and we will replace the holy water. Mayhap Gwinith will be delivered of her babe soon. It would be well to be prepared."

I called next at Father Robert's vicarage. Piers answered my knock and invited me to enter. He knew where I had been, and before I could ask of Father Robert he asked of the new lock.

"'Tis in place now, as we speak," I said. "Father Thomas and Father Ralph will replace the holy water this day."

"Ah . . . so this troubling business is ended," the clerk said.

"Not completely. There is yet the matter of Father Robert's attack."

"You believe the felon who did that may yet be discovered?"

"I do. If not, 'twill not be for want of effort. Lord Gilbert pays me to keep order upon his manor. Swatting a priest upon his head is nothing if not disorderly. Now, I would see Father Robert and learn how he fares."

He did not fare well. I saw no improvement since last I called. He was alert and his wits were sound, but he moved only his dexter arm and leg. While on the road to and from Oxford I had thought more on the matter of atrophied muscles and that they might require stimulation before they would again obey commands.

I called Piers to me and showed him what must be done. "First take his arm and move it side to side, up and down. Do this over and again, many times. Thrice each day. Then Father Robert must lay upon his bed whilst you raise his leg. Raise it so that his toes point to the ceiling. Do this over and again three times each day."

Would these exercises do any good? I did not know. Henri de Mondeville did not mention such a practice, but I didn't think such exercise could do harm. When I demonstrated to Piers what he should do, Father Robert had not complained of discomfort. Was this good? Or did the lack of feeling foretell a future in which the priest would never control his sinister arm and leg?

The pebble! As I departed Father Robert's vicarage it came to me that, in the joy of fitting the new lock to St. Beornwald's font, I had not heard the small stone slide from the lid to the flags. Had I been too excited to notice, or had the pebble already been displaced? I upbraided myself for my lack of attention.

I hurried back to the church, peered behind the font, and readily found the displaced pebble. But when had it fallen from the lid? This day, when Father Thomas and I tried the new lock? Nay, Father Thomas had not lifted the font lid; he'd merely tried the new lock. Some earlier time? There was a man who might know: the holy man.

Bampton's holy man had appeared in the town many years past. He was first seen squatting at the corner where Church View Street joins Bridge Street. His custom was to place a hand upon the heads of children who passed by and mouth a silent prayer. At first parents were displeased at his familiar behavior, but soon opinion turned in his favor as his actions proved benign.

He never spoke, and after many hours of questions, which he would answer with a nod or shake of his head, I learned why. He had gone on pilgrimage to Compostela, became lost, gone astray, and found himself in Grenada, where Mussulmen enslaved him. When he would not confess Mohammed as God's prophet, they tore out his tongue for heresy.

The man eventually managed to escape his captors and make his way back to England, where he hoped to attach himself to a monastery as a lay brother. But, due to his deformity, no house would have him. He wandered the realm, eventually discovering an abandoned swineherd's hut a short distance west of Bampton Castle. Lord Gilbert did not drive him from the forest, as he did no man harm.

The holy man now resides in a small house, which Lord Gilbert had built for him after he aided me in the capture of a felon. This he was able to do because several times each week he would prowl Bampton's streets after curfew. At first this displeased me, but I came to consider that eyes and ears alert in the night might be a good thing. Had the holy man seen some fellow lurking about St. Beornwald's Church in the night? A man intent on stealing holy water?

'Twas nearly time for supper when I approached the holy man's tiny cottage. Smoke from the gable vents told me he was likely simmering pottage for his supper. So he was.

In return for blessing their children, folk of Bampton and the Weald are generous with charity. He often receives eggs, sacks of peas, beans, and oats. Even occasionally a small portion of bacon.

The door stood open to the mild afternoon breeze, and when I called – in the four years the holy man had resided in Bampton I have never learned his name – he appeared. The holy man never begins a conversation. How could he? His part in a conversation consists only of the movement of his head. Nods and shakes. Although at times I wonder if the man could not make himself understood if he tried to speak.

I greeted the man and asked if he had heard of the disappearance of holy water from St. Beornwald's font.

He nodded. I suppose if there is an advantage to being unable to speak it is that one listens well.

"A new lock has been fitted to the font this day, so the holy water is now safe. But the man who struck down Father Robert is still at large. In the past month have you walked the streets after curfew and seen another man doing the same? Especially near the church?"

The holy man shook his head.

It has become known in Bampton that the holy man may be seen after curfew, and that John, the beadle, has been told to ignore the violation. Did this mean that the man who struck down Father Robert was of Bampton, and knew the holy man's practice so that he could avoid him? If so, what of the barrel stave from Witney? Surely a man could find a likely club in Lord Gilbert's forest.

"When the thief learns that a new lock protects St. Beornwald's holy water he will probably give up his larceny," I said, "or practice it some other place where the font is not so well protected. Nevertheless, when you prowl Bampton's streets at night, keep an eye upon the church."

The holy man nodded agreement and I released him to go to his meal. I was eager for my own supper, and when I returned to Galen House was pleased to find that Kate and Adela had prepared sops dory. Bessie was also pleased, as 'tis a meal she much enjoys. So much so that she is occasionally silent so as to better keep her mouth full.

Friday morning, after breaking my fast, I sought Father Robert's vicarage to learn if the exercises I had assigned had improved the priest's condition. They had not. I am impatient about such matters. When I set a broken arm or stitch closed a wound, I want to see healing next day. A man's body, with skillful aid, will heal. Usually. But not rapidly.

"I've done as you requested," Piers said. "Father Robert does not complain when I move his arm and leg. Says it doesn't cause him pain. That's good, is it not?"

"I don't know. It may be that some discomfort would be good. When a man tries to lift a burden too great for him, he will often feel an ache."

"You want me to lift and tug on Father Robert's arm and leg 'til he complains?"

"Nay. I see no point in causing him to suffer when the outcome is in doubt."

This conversation ended abruptly when a vigorous thumping rattled the vicarage door. Piers looked to me with curiosity in his eyes, then hurried to the door.

I heard a voice ask if I was within.

"Aye," Piers said. "He called to learn how Father Robert does."

"Father Thomas is at the church and begs Sir Hugh to attend him straightaway."

I recognized the voice. 'Twas Gerard's. I could not guess why I might be summoned to St. Beornwald's Church on a Friday morning. The bell announcing the dawn Angelus had sounded nearly an hour past. Mayhap, I thought, one of the elderly worshipers had fallen ill. Or simply fallen.

"What has happened?" I asked.

"The font . . . come and see."

I looked to Father Robert, shrugged, and set off behind Gerard. The clerk hurried to the church and plunged through the porch into the south aisle. The rising sun illuminated this area and I saw Father Thomas wringing his hands over the font. The lid was thrown back. The priest was clearly disturbed. Father Ralph looked on with mouth agape.

"Ah, Sir Hugh, you are come. Lady Katherine said you could be found at Father Robert's vicarage. It has happened again."

"What has?"

"The font. 'Tis dry."

"You and Father Ralph filled it yesterday?"

"We did. Today, after the dawn Angelus, I decided to try the new lock again. I was like a lad with a new toy."

"It worked well?"

"Aye. I unlocked the font, and on a whim decided to look under the lid. 'Twas dry, as if Father Ralph and I had not filled it and consecrated the water. There must be an undiscovered leak somewhere in the basin."

"We have already ruled that out," I said. "The lead of the basin is unmarred, and there is no moisture at the base of the font where leaking water would accumulate from a crack in the basin."

"But there must be a leak. How else could the font be dry this morning when it was full last night?"

"It was unlocked," I said.

Father Thomas and Father Ralph looked to each other, dumbfounded.

"How could such a thing be?" Father Thomas finally said. "I have the key and it was in my chamber all last night. Father Ralph, Father Robert, and I have not yet decided where it would best be kept."

"There is another key," I replied.

"Another? Who has it?"

"I do not know. But if the font does not leak – and we

know it doesn't – and you had the key in your chamber last night, then there must be another key."

"Mayhap," Father Ralph said, "some man crept into your vicarage in the night and made off with the key."

"Bah!" Father Thomas replied. "Gerard bars the door each night. And if some scoundrel did manage to enter in the night, how would he find the key in the dark? And if he did find it, he'd have to return to the vicarage to replace it."

"Father Thomas speaks true," I said. "No man entered his vicarage to take the key. The man who made the lock made a second key for it, and that key is now in the possession of the rogue who has been seizing holy water."

"Can such an accusation be proven?" Father Thomas said. "The locksmith will certainly claim not."

"Aye. There is little point in asking the fellow if he made two keys," I said. "He will deny it. Only if we can find the man who has the second key will we be able to prove the locksmith's duplicity."

"The locksmith will know that we know of his second key," Gerard said.

"Likely," I replied. "He would be a dolt not to know that we suspect a second key."

"Will the thief return to take more water?" Father Thomas said.

"If you fill it again, and he knows of it, he probably will."

"So the font must remain dry, or we must set a watch as before."

"Setting a watch did not succeed," I said. "I suppose we might have two men watch every night, but if the scoundrel learns of it he will shun the church 'til we grow weary of the watch."

"How would the thief know if two men awaited his appearance?" Father Ralph asked.

"He might not," I said, "but gossip travels where truth fears to tread. And there may be a way to watch for the man but not watch at the same time."

This statement was greeted with silence and incomprehension. I did not explain. I had the holy man's nocturnal roaming in mind, but would not say so, even to priests and clerks. I was beginning to trust no man.

"How will you do that?" Father Thomas said. "Watch yet not watch?"

"Some day I may tell you, but not today. For today, leave the font dry, as before. Lock the lid. If the font is empty it will not matter. The thief will think the holy water renewed. As for me, I am hungry. I am going to Galen House and my dinner."

Chapter 9

Kate and Adela had prepared a pottage of whelks and apple moise. As fast day meals go, such a repast is as tasty as a man might want. But before I could set to my trencher, Kate wanted to know why Gerard had sought me earlier.

"The font is empty again."

Adela was bustling about the kitchen and I was sure she heard. By tomorrow, folk in Bampton and the Weald would know.

"But the lock . . ." Kate said. "Did Father Thomas forget to lock the lid?"

"Nay. It was locked."

"How could this be?"

"You ask the same question Father Thomas and Father Ralph and the clerks asked. 'Tis my belief there is another key."

"The locksmith made two keys," she said. "He would only do so if paid."

"Aye, and paid well."

"But if you confront him he will deny all."

"He will."

"What will you do?"

I did not reply, but glanced to Adela, whose back was at that moment turned, then looked to Bessie and John. Kate nodded understanding and let the matter drop. For the remainder of the meal we discussed the weather, which was good, and the poll tax, which was not.

Collecting the poll tax weighed heavily on me as I walked past the castle to the holy man's cottage. Parliament had decreed that professional beggars were exempt from the poll tax. Did that include the holy man? He had no source of income and did no work, but subsisted upon the charity of Bampton folk – although I'd not heard of the man ever asking for alms or other benefactions. Did his state make him a beggar or not? Whatever I decided, neither the king nor Prince John would know, so I would not concern myself with the matter. Lord Gilbert could decide.

I seem always to seek the holy man when he is about the business of preparing or consuming a meal. His dinner this day was simmering in a pot, and its greenish consistency indicated that he had recently been the recipient of a sack of peas.

The fellow tugged a forelock as I approached, and waited for me to speak.

"Did you walk Bampton's streets last night?" I asked.

He shook his head.

"I wish for you to do so this night and every night for the next week. Pay close attention to the church. If you see a man near the church, follow him. Keep to the shadows so he will not know you are behind. When you learn where the man has gone, come to Galen House and awaken me."

He nodded that he understood.

I did not expect to be awakened this night. Whoso took the holy water would likely assume that the font had not yet been refilled, or would hear the gossip and know that the font would not be filled. Why return to an empty font? Mayhap a trap might catch the fellow. Would he seek holy water if he thought the supply was replenished?

From the holy man's hut I walked to Father Thomas's vicarage. I stopped at the bridge over Shill Brook to consider my scheme. The matter seemed simple enough: over the next few days, have word bandied about that St. Beornwald's font was refilled, then wait to see if the holy man saw anyone enter the church after curfew.

Father Thomas approved of the plan, likely because he had no better idea as to what might be done about vanishing holy water.

"You want me to wait a few days before I replace the holy water?" the priest asked.

"You need not replace it at all. It is needful only that the thief believes you have done so."

"You ask me to lie? I should then be as great a sinner as the thief."

"Will a falsehood told for a good reason send a man to hell?" I asked.

"I would prefer not to learn if it would."

"What of the Hebrew midwives?"

"Who?"

"Pharaoh told them to slay all the male babes born to Hebrew women. They did not, and when he discovered this and pressed them about it, they claimed that Hebrew women gave birth so easily the babes were delivered before the midwives could attend the births."

"Oh . . . I remember."

"This was a lie, but God did not punish the midwives. Rather, they were rewarded."

"You suggest the Lord Christ will reward me if I tell this lie?"

"Not in the same way the Hebrew midwives were rewarded. They were given families."

"Hah! I'd not consider that a reward. 'Twould be the result of another sin."

"Today is Friday. Who will preach the homily Sunday? You, or Father Ralph?"

"Father Ralph."

"By Sunday I suspect all folk will know that the holy water has been stolen again. Suggest to Father Ralph that he allude to it having been replaced."

As on Friday, after breaking my fast on Saturday I sought Father Robert's vicarage. Piers admitted me and I found the priest consuming a maslin loaf and in remarkably good spirits, considering his affliction.

"I pray daily that I will regain normal use of hand and foot," the priest said. "But if I do not, I am content. St. Paul wrote that he asked the Lord Christ three times to remove some affliction, but He did not. Who am I to receive a blessing denied to the apostle?"

"Does it cause you pain when Piers extends your arm and leg?"

"Nay . . . well, not much."

"Perhaps that is a good sign," I said. "Often pain is how a man's body tells him to stop doing that which causes the hurt. But not always. A man becomes a stronger runner when he runs until he feels discomfort and then continues to run."

"Discomfort," Father Robert said. "Aye, that is what I feel after Piers tugs at my arm and leg."

"Not pain?"

"Nay. I will pray, as did the apostle, to be made whole, but meanwhile Piers can continue his labors."

Sunday morning at mass, as planned, Father Ralph's homily included a reference to St. Beornwald's font and the renewed holy water within. Evidently, Father Ralph did not consider this tale a mortal sin – or Father Thomas had reminded him of the Hebrew midwives.

The announcement of the font's refilled basin did not seem to elicit amazement from the parishioners. I watched to see if any showed surprise. Of course, I could not see the faces of the entire congregation, but those I observed seemed credulous.

Father Thomas blessed the pax board and sent it through the congregation. Most kissed it enthusiastically. Would a man do so if he was guilty of taking holy water from the font? Probably. A man who commits enough felonies will eventually become inured to the practice. I have treated many folk who come to me in pain – so many that the agony of broken bones or the suffering of a severe laceration no longer troubles me. I simply set to work to mend and heal. Is this how miscreants feel about their felonies? Another in a long list, and forgettable?

My sleep was not interrupted for the next two nights, although it might as well have been, as I placed my head upon the pillow expecting to be awakened and slept fitfully.

I awoke Wednesday, June 24, to an incessant thumping upon Galen House door. 'Twas Lord Gilbert's nephew and page, Charles de Burgh. The lad had evidently been instructed to hurry, for he stood at the threshold red-faced and panting.

"Lord Gilbert requires your presence," he gasped. "'Tis the king . . . he is dead."

Kate stood behind me as the child spoke, so heard all. "What does Lord Gilbert want of you regarding this matter?" she said to me.

"We are to have a boy king," I said. "Richard of Bordeaux is but ten years old. There are, among his relatives, several, I'm sure, who would like to supplant him."

"His uncle, John?" Kate said as Charles slipped off down Church View Street.

"Principally," I said. "Although the lad's mother has known this day would soon come, so I'm sure she has been securing adherents to guard against usurpation."

"Is Lord Gilbert one of these, do you suppose?"

"Mayhap. I'd be surprised if partisans of both camps had not sought his allegiance. He can command many knights and men-at-arms."

"What does he want of you?"

"Whatever it is, he is not to be kept waiting. I'm off to the castle."

I had not taken ten steps from my door when I saw the holy man approach from Bridge Street. His pace was that of a man on a mission, intent on completing his task forthwith. His cast-off robe flapped about his ankles, and he seemed about to break into a run.

I met him near the intersection of Rosemary Lane and Church View Street. He was agitated, and I knew his appearance meant he had information for me. About some tenebrous visitor to St. Beornwald's Church?

That knowledge must wait. I told the holy man that I was called to the castle, and that he should return to his hut and I would seek him there when I had completed Lord Gilbert's business. He nodded and together we retraced his steps, crossed Shill Brook, passed the mill, and when I diverged into the castle forecourt he continued to his home.

When called to Lord Gilbert's presence I usually found him in the solar, so I hurried directly to the steps leading to that chamber. I had rapped but once upon the door when John Chamberlain opened to me. He was clearly expecting my arrival.

"Ah, Sir Hugh," Lord Gilbert exclaimed. "Did Charles tell you the news?"

"King Edward is dead."

"Aye. Died Sunday at Sheen Palace. Word is that Mistress Alice stripped the rings from his fingers before he was cold."

"What of the poll tax?" I said. "With the king dead and a ten-year-old boy about to take the throne, surely Prince John does not intend to send an army to France."

"Hah! Don't be too sure of that. Or of a boy king, for that matter." Lord Gilbert saw my expression and continued. "Lady Joan desires my presence in Westminster. And not mine alone. She has called for others to attend Richard's coronation. Of course, most barons would do so even if not asked. She fears, I believe, that an empty throne will attract many rumps."

"Prince John's?"

"The man is not popular, but has designs – as we who know him know all too well. Until Richard is safely crowned at Westminster, Prince John must be carefully watched. He'd like nothing more than to seize the throne and see his son, Henry Bolingbroke, succeed him."

"Henry is the same age as Richard, is he not?"

"Aye. Only a few months separate them. So tomorrow I am off to Westminster with knights and men-at-arms. I will not return until after Richard's coronation. I leave you in charge of Bampton Manor.

"Now, on another matter. Word has come to me that the font in St. Beornwald's Church was found empty again, even after a new lock was made for the lid."

"Aye. There is much amiss to do with holy water. And

not only here in Bampton. Holy water has also been taken from St. Mary's Church in Witney."

"Well, mayhap you will have sorted the matter out by the time I return from London."

"When will that be?"

"Who can say? Soon, I hope. Before those who would deny the throne to Richard can plot some mischief. Which they are likely doing as we speak."

Lord Gilbert dismissed me and turned to his chamberlain to make preparations for the journey to Westminster. This was no concern of mine, so I departed the solar and hurried to the holy man's hut to learn of the information he had been eager to impart.

It was the third hour, but as usual the holy man had pottage bubbling upon his hearthstone. I hoped for something more savory for my own dinner, but as I had consumed no loaf to break my fast, the scent of the holy man's gruel set my stomach to growling.

"Have you news for me?" I asked.

He nodded.

"Did you walk the streets last night?"

Another nod.

"Did you see a man near the church?"

He nodded again.

"Were you able to follow him?"

He nodded, but then raised his hands, palms up, as if to indicate confusion.

"You were not able to follow the fellow to his home?"

He nodded again.

The moon had been past full and rose late in the night. Mayhap the man skulking about the church did so when he knew he would not have moonlight to contend with. I asked the holy man.

"Did you see the fellow early in the night, before the moon arose?"

He nodded.

"So you could not see well enough to follow the man to some house in Bampton or the Weald?"

He nodded, then pointed to the path which led to the road. He evidently wished to show me something.

"Lead on," I said.

The fire under his pot had burned low. He carefully scattered the ashes, then set off through the wood. 'Twas a warm day, and unless what he wished me to see would take a long while he could yet have a hot dinner.

The holy man would, I expected, direct me to some street in Bampton or the Weald where he'd lost sight of his quarry. He did not. He strode purposefully to Church View Street, past Galen House and the church, and set off up the Witney road. After a few hundred paces he stopped and pointed north, in the direction of Lew and Witney.

"You followed a man last night to this place?" I asked.

Could this have been the holy water thief? Was it the man who struck down Father Robert? If so, he was not of Bampton or the Weald. But he had committed his felonies – some of them, at least – in my bailiwick, and it was therefore my duty to see the man apprehended.

"Did the fellow carry anything?" I asked. "An ewer, perhaps, or a bladder in which he might carry some liquid?"

The holy man raised his palms and shrugged to indicate ignorance.

If the holy water thief had come to Bampton to fill his flask, he had departed disappointed. Which did not mean he would not return some night. Men love darkness rather than light when their deeds are evil.

We returned to Galen House, where I sent the holy man to his dinner and went eagerly to my own. Kate and Adela had prepared a charlet of cod, and between bites I told them of Lord Gilbert's summons and the duty he had assigned me.

"You think Lady Joan will need armed men to seat her son upon the throne?" Kate asked.

"If she has enough supporters she will need none," I replied.

"Ah, if she had few," Kate said, "she would face a stronger threat than if she had many."

"Just so. Now, on another matter, the holy man followed a man prowling about St. Beornwald's Church last night."

"Where did he go?"

"North, on the road to Witney."

"Then you seek a man not of Bampton?"

"Evidently. And I will have to do the searching on my own. Lord Gilbert will take Sir Jaket, Thomas, Janyn, and mayhap even Uctred, when he travels to London. A few grooms of the marshalsea may remain to care for the beasts he leaves at the castle."

Kate frowned at this thought. "If the thief is the same who battered Father Robert, he will not hesitate to do the same to you."

"Perhaps. But Father Robert was caught unaware. I, on the other hand, expect the worst, which is the only safe strategy for a bailiff."

"What little good that may do," Kate scoffed.

Witney is but five miles from Bampton, and the days were now long. I could walk there and be home before dark. To what purpose? There are likely five hundred men in Witney. How could I determine which had visited Bampton in the night? Look for eyes red from lack of sleep?

If I did decide to visit Witney, there would be a few runcies and palfries remaining at the castle marshalsea. Riding would be better than walking, even if the horses left at the castle were old and long of tooth. However I traveled to Witney, the same conundrum would await me: how to discover among a town full of men which had come to Bampton in the night.

Roads are not safe, as my Kate continually reminds me. The man who came from Witney to Bampton in the night did so at some risk. Or did he travel with an accomplice or two? It would not be necessary for two or three men to enter St. Beornwald's Church to fill a container with holy water. The companions could have waited along the road whilst one man did the felony. If the holy man had followed the thief another hundred or so paces from Bampton, would he have seen a felon's companions appear in the shadows of the verge?

What if I waited at some place where the forest came close to the road? But not alone. Mayhap Uctred would remain behind when Lord Gilbert set off for Westminster the next day. Uctred is not young, but he is as tough as old leather. And the three clerks of St. Beornwald's could add up to a small force. In the dark, a rogue could not identify them as scholars rather than robust plowmen.

I finished my dinner and went to the castle. I wished to learn two things: would Uctred travel with Lord Gilbert the next day, and would a few horses remain behind?

Chapter 10

Uctred was to remain, and seven beasts, also. The horses would be useless for what I had planned, although if three men appeared on the Witney road, a horse or two might help to run down any escapee. The clerks would be of no use, none of them able to run farther than a hundred paces before gasping for breath and turning red in the face. Uctred would be willing, but his form defines the term "bandy-legged". It would be up to me to chase any man who fled from the ambush, and I am not so fleet as I once was. Kate's cookery has much to do with this.

I found Uctred helping the marshalsea prepare the beasts which would carry the knights to Westminster. He seemed dismayed that he was not to accompany the party and was cheered when I briefly explained the duty I had in mind for him.

"When you goin' to set this ambush?" he asked.

"Friday evening. In the meantime, I'll set the vicars to announcing at the Angelus that St. Beornwald's font has been refilled."

Would such a disclosure reach Witney by Friday? Only if some man of Bampton heard it and relayed the news. This business was becoming complicated. The holy water thief was of Witney, but either he was receiving information from some man of Bampton or the Weald, or I'd missed my guess.

From the castle I walked to Father Robert's vicarage. I needed to tell Piers what was desired of him Friday evening, and observe Father Robert's condition.

The clerk did not seem pleased that he was asked to lose a night's sleep, and my authority was not great enough to command that he do so. But Father Robert heard my request and agreed that Piers should take part in the ambush.

The plaster skullcap I had made for the priest was beginning to crumble about the edges. And Father Robert complained that his scalp would sometimes itch but he could not relieve the prickle with a good scratching.

"The plaster should remain," I said, "for another week. Your skull was cracked just more than three weeks past. I would feel better about its mending if the break were protected for another week. Now, as to your sinister arm and leg, are you able to command some movement?"

"Piers requires that I submit to his pulling and tugging three times each day, as you instructed."

"Is the practice of some benefit?"

"Aye, I believe so. If I rise from bed or bench I must have support or my leg will cause me to tumble. Yet I do think it stronger than a week past. Mayhap 'tis my imagination. I hope for a thing, so come to believe it so."

I have sometimes wondered if such an attitude might speed healing. If a man believes himself to be mending, will such presumption actually improve his recovery? De Mondeville and Galen were silent on the subject.

Neither Gerard nor Martyn were any more enthusiastic than Piers about hiding through the night at the edge of a dark forest. But Father Thomas and Father Ralph thought an ambush a good idea, so that settled the matter. Father Thomas agreed to tell those who attended the dawn

Angelus on Thursday that the font was filled and ready to be of service when the next infant had need of it.

Most who attend the dawn Angelus are elderly, enjoy gossip, and may be relied upon to spread news through the town. If my supposition was correct, sometime late Thursday or Friday some man of Bampton or the Weald would take the report to Witney.

The Lord Christ might have looked with favor upon my scheme and provided a clear, dry night. He did not. Shortly after midnight Saturday morning rain began to fall, and by the time the waning moon provided faint illumination, we five were soaked to the skin.

Nights are short in June. I did not believe my quarry would risk the dawn, so when the eastern sky began to lighten I called off the watch and sent my companions home. They did not find this disagreeable. Nor did I. Mayhap the rain which drenched us persuaded the Witney felon – or felons – to try the road on a less muddy night.

"Meet again tonight at Galen House," I said as my companions set off through the mire for castle and vicarages. "Unless 'tis yet raining. I suspect the felon we seek did not appear because he preferred a warm, dry bed to collecting more holy water."

Saturday night the rain had become a soft mist. The foliage was wet. We kept the watch and became nearly as damp as the previous night. The road was still muddy, but I did not believe this would hinder a dedicated thief. Something did, for the road was empty of life, but for a lone fox which appeared just before dawn. The animal suspected there were men about. His nose twitched and his head swiveled. He finally identified the place from which our scent came, and trotted off in the other direction. The appearance of the fox was the only diversion on what was otherwise a boring night.

Was there any reason to continue the watch for a third night? If the felon thought the holy water replenished but had not returned to help himself, mayhap he had enough for whatever vile purpose he pursued. I told Uctred and the clerks we would discontinue the watch until there was better reason to resume it.

As usual, Kate and I did not break our fast Sunday morning, contenting ourselves with a cup of ale. So I was hungry and sleepy and found it difficult to keep my chin from my chest when Father Ralph spoke the homily. I noticed that the clerks had the same problem. I also noticed that Piers was alone. Father Robert did not attend the mass. He was probably self-conscious about his feeble state.

Could I follow a man to Witney safely? To suggest so would incur Kate's displeasure, but requiring Uctred and the three clerks to lay in wait for a man who might or might not appear seemed foolish.

After a dinner of lozenges de chare I set off for the holy man's hut. He had already consumed his dinner, so this visit did not interrupt his cookery.

"Have you walked the streets in the night since I last called on you?" I asked.

He shook his head.

"Do you intend to do so soon?"

He nodded.

"Tonight?"

He nodded again.

"If you see a man tonight about the church, do not follow him, but come straightaway to Galen House and tell me."

He nodded agreement.

"And if you see no man this night, but do Monday or Tuesday, do the same. Come immediately to Galen House."

On my way to Galen House I called at the castle. The place was quiet, most of its inhabitants now on the road to Westminster. I sought Uctred, and when I found him he leaped to the wrong conclusion.

"We going to lay in wait again?" he asked.

"Nay. Doing so was unproductive. I have instructed the holy man to keep watch over St. Beornwald's Church in the night, and this time come immediately to Galen House if he sees a man near the church after curfew. Kate will be distressed if I follow such a man or try to apprehend him alone, so I'd like for you to sleep at Galen House for a few nights. Bring your dagger. If but one man is our quarry, I will arrest him – for defying curfew if nothing else. If two or more are about in the dark, we will follow. To Witney, likely."

Uctred arrived at dusk and I placed him on a pallet in the chamber I use for treating those who need my surgical skills. He was soon snoring. Not so loudly as Arthur once did, but the rumble carried up the stairs well enough that I despaired of sleep myself. I had nearly decided that the arrangement was a poor idea when Morpheus finally overcame me.

The holy man did not disturb my slumber Sunday evening, but shortly before dawn Tuesday morning a rapping upon Galen House door awakened me. I knew who must be at the door.

Uctred was also awakened and we reached the door at the same time. 'Twas indeed the holy man. He stood silently in the dark, awaiting the questions which always began our conversations.

"You have seen a man near the church?" I asked.

The holy man nodded.

"Did he enter the church?"

He nodded again.

"Is he yet there?"

He shook his head.

"Is he on the road to Witney?"

I was surprised at the holy man's response. He shook his head.

"He has not remained in the church, yet is not on the road to Witney?" I said. "Where has the fellow gone? Did you follow?"

He nodded, then pointed toward Church Street. He intended that Uctred and I follow. We did.

The holy man led us to Church Street, thence to Broad Street and from there east toward St. Andrew's Chapel. This was all wrong. The holy water thief was from Witney. Or were there two felons dealing in purloined holy water; two involved in sacrilege and the black arts? Witney was to the north. The holy man led us to the Eynsham road.

A bird in the hand is worth two in the bush. I decided that Uctred and I would follow this new quarry, so I thanked the holy man for his service and dismissed him. Somewhere along the road to Eynsham, if we hurried, we might come upon the felon.

We had traveled perhaps two hundred paces beyond St. Andrew's Chapel when the sound of distant hoofbeats came to my ears. If the man we followed had mounted a horse we would not catch him, for the beast had been spurred to a gallop. The sound diminished as we stood in the road, the rider beyond apprehension.

"Lost 'im," Uctred said. "You suppose 'e had an 'orse tethered on the verge, ready to flee?"

"Aye. He'd not risk riding the beast through the town. He'd surely be heard."

"Think mayhap 'e had a partner waitin' for 'im, keepin' the 'orse?"

"I heard only one horse galloping away."

"Aye. Didn't sound like two horses," Uctred said.

We were stymied, and there was nothing left to us but to return to Bampton. We did, and the rising sun illuminated the saints carved at the base of St. Beornwald's tower before we reached Church View Street.

Kate had heard me depart in the night and was eager to know the reason. I explained as Uctred and I broke our fast with maslin loaves and ale.

"So there are two felons taking holy water from St. Beornwald's font?" Kate concluded when I finished the tale. "Unless the man who was seen going north, on the road to Witney, had nothing to do with the missing holy water."

"Unlikely," I said.

"The holy man told you that the miscreant you followed last night had entered the church, did he not? Did he say the same about the man who departed Bampton on the Witney road?"

"Nay."

"Then perhaps that man had nothing to do with the stolen holy water."

"Mayhap," I said. "But to be upon the streets so late, after curfew, surely means he was up to no good."

"Aye," Kate agreed. "There are likely many reasons a man might violate curfew having nothing to do with the theft of holy water; most of them, however, having to do with some disreputable business."

"Which means the matter falls within my bailiwick, even if the man's nocturnal habits have nothing to do with dry fonts and stolen holy water."

"If a man has honorable business, he'll go about it in the daytime," Uctred said. "Question is, was the fellow from Bampton, goin' to Witney for some shady dealings, or t'other way round . . . bein' from Witney an' come to Bampton for some fishy business?"

Gilbert, young as he was, had developed excellent lungs and discovered that the use of them would bring gustatory satisfaction. When we heard the babe, Kate rose from the table and climbed the stairs to answer the child's demand. Adela began preparation for dinner, and Bessie and John went to the toft to entertain themselves.

"You going to ask the holy man to keep watch again?" Uctred said.

"To what purpose? If the thief came again we would need to be mounted to catch him, and Lord Gilbert did not leave fleet horses behind. The beasts which remain are old and slow, and near to being food for the hounds."

"Then what is to be done?"

I had no ready answer. Whatever scheme I tried in order to find the holy water thief failed, and in one case had led to the injury of a priest. Perhaps a permanent injury. 'Twas as if some men knew my thoughts before I did and could put them to practice.

As a last, desperate measure, a visit to John Tey might prove worthwhile. Could I bluster and rant enough that the fellow would admit to making a second key for the lock on St. Beornwald's font? A key which he had sold to some man who had used it to continue stealing holy water? Mayhap the locksmith might even know the use to which the purloined holy water was put.

I did not relish another visit to Oxford, but had no other strategy which had not already been tried and found wanting.

"Return to the castle and have the marshalsea prepare two palfreys for tomorrow." I said.

"Where we goin'?"

"Oxford. To visit a conniving locksmith."

Wednesday morning I broke my fast with a wheaten loaf and ale, and reminded Kate that she must bar the doors securely if I did not return by nightfall. I hoped that I might, as the days were long. On the other hand, the palfreys Uctred and I would ride were old and slow. That could not be helped.

Uctred appeared with the palfreys as I finished my ale, and after a kiss from Kate I set off for Oxford. We passed through Eynsham in little more than an hour, but after Swinford the palfreys became fatigued and the last miles to Oxford were slow.

We stabled the beasts at the Fox and Hounds, and I gave the stable boy tuppence to provide two buckets of oats. The inn offered a pottage of whelks for dinner, and after a meal of the chewy creatures we set off for St. Mildred's Street and John Tey's shop.

We found the establishment closed and shuttered. The front door was fastened with one of Tey's locks. I saw his initials embossed on it. The rear door was apparently barred. I banged loudly on it and called the locksmith's name. To no effect. The situation was a duplicate of my earlier visit three weeks past.

Mayhap the herbalist next door would know where Tey had gone, or when he would return. He did not, and seemed surprised that the locksmith was not tending to business.

The glover on the opposite side of Tey's shop was more helpful. "Opened 'is shutters this mornin', like always, then closed up an' went off with some customer. In a hurry, like."

A customer, or an informant? Had some man known when we departed Bampton five hours past where we were going, and why? 'Twas possible an informant told the holy water thief when St. Beornwald's font was filled and when it was dry. Why did I suspect such a thing? Because no matter my scheme to apprehend the holy water thief, some man seemed to perceive my intent. And also because bailiffs become suspicious of everyone and everything. I take that back. I have no suspicions about my Kate.

It was surely possible that the locksmith had gone off with a potential customer to examine some door or chest which required security. In that case he would return, I guessed, in an hour or so. But even if his return was prompt, we would not see Bampton before dark. Not to worry. Abbot Gerleys of Eynsham Abbey always welcomes me if I need a bed and am unable to continue my journey to Bampton.

By the ninth hour I was persuaded that wherever Tey had gone, and for whatever reason, he did not intend to return to his shop this day. Should I return to Bampton, my mission a failure? There was enough time to reach Eynsham and the abbey, no matter the weary state of our beasts.

Sheriff de Elmerugg was certainly off to Westminster with a flock of knights and men-at-arms. There would be empty chambers at Oxford Castle this night. I had met several of the sheriff's serjeants and constables. Perhaps one of these was left in charge of the castle. Uctred and I might prevail upon the man for a night's lodging. So it was, and we were once again spared combat with the fleas and lice at the Fox and Hounds.

The locksmith would not abandon his business on consecutive days. Or would he? Mayhap, if he were paid enough to do so. But how would he know I was here to seek him? And was the practice of black arts so profitable that Tey would abjure his business for two days? Was money involved? Or did men want holy water for its own sake, having nothing to do with pence and shillings?

As with most Oxford burghers, the locksmith lived above his shop. Uctred and I departed the castle at dawn, intending to catch Tey as he opened for business. We did not, for his shop remained shuttered all morning. Neither the herbalist nor the glover knew where the locksmith might have gone. Or if they did, they feigned ignorance, as they had the day before.

Uctred and I shared a roasted capon at the Fox and Hounds, retrieved our palfreys, and paid the stable boy another tuppence for oats. Our beasts were old and slow, but age had done nothing to dull their appetites. They had consumed four buckets of oats, and according to the stable boy would have devoured four more had they been given the opportunity. We then set out across Bookbinders' Bridge for home.

I've had, in past years, many discomfiting experiences when crossing the Thames at Swinford. These adventures have affected me, so when Uctred and I approached the ford I became alert. *More* alert, I should say, for any man who travels the roads these days is alert. Safety requires it, even of two men.

So it was that as our beasts were about to step into the current, I looked to my dexter side and saw a face peering at us through the underbrush. When the fellow saw that I noticed him, he instantly disappeared. I was about to ask Uctred if he had seen or possibly recognized the man, but remembered that his eyes were weak.

We might have halted our journey and set off through the wood to learn who this watcher was. Was he a potential thief, seeking a solitary traveler he might rob? Or mayhap a solitary traveler who had heard us approach and left the road, deciding discretion better than valor?

I told Uctred of the sighting as we splashed across the river. We stopped part way across to allow the palfreys to drink, passed the gatehouse to Eynsham Abbey without stopping, and arrived in Bampton in time for supper. Where Church View Street meets Bridge Street I dismounted, sent Uctred to the castle with the beasts, and walked to Galen House.

Adela had already departed for her home in the Weald, so Kate and I consumed our supper and enjoyed conversation without concern that our opinions would be bandied about. Of course, Bessie might serve the same purpose. Not so much John.

"Oh, I nearly forgot," Kate said as we finished our supper. "The holy man called this morning. As you were away, I questioned him and learned that he wants to see you."

"Soon?" I said.

"I believe so. He seemed somewhat agitated."

"I will seek him now, before nightfall."

Chapter 11

The long twilight of midsummer lighted my way to the holy man's hut. The gentle breeze, the birds calling to one another as they prepared to roost for the night, the scent of honeysuckle – all these served to erase the melancholy I felt due to the failed journey to Oxford. I hoped that whatever the holy man had to tell me would not spoil an otherwise pleasant evening.

It did not, although when I first learned of his information I thought it might.

The holy man had moved his bench out of the hut and, like many folk of Bampton and the Weald, was enjoying a fine evening.

"You sought me at Galen House this morning. Did you learn something last night whilst walking the streets?"

He nodded.

"Another man lurking near the church?"

Another nod.

"Did this man enter the church?"

This time the holy man shook his head.

"Then I will hazard a guess that he departed Bampton to the north, on the road to Witney, as before. The man you saw enter the church went east, toward Eynsham. Did the fellow go north?"

Another nod.

I was perplexed. How could a man steal holy water if he did not enter the church? But the man who entered the church seeking holy water did not leave Bampton going toward Witney, as I was convinced he should, but rather went east and mounted a horse only a short distance east of St. Andrew's Chapel. If the rogue who left Bampton on the Witney road did not enter St. Beornwald's Church, how could he secure holy water from the font? Did he break curfew for some other reason?

The man who departed Bampton in the night, bound for Witney, seemed to do so on a fairly regular schedule. If this was so, he might be on the road again in a few days. Could I follow in the dark and learn where he went? Uctred, with his failing eyes, would be of no help. Better to allow the old fellow to remain abed. As for me, I would wait until dark Saturday evening, then find some deeply shadowed place beyond St. Beornwald's Church to wait and watch. Waiting and watching had become a significant pastime.

Kate opposed this scheme, as I knew she would. I told her my intention was but to follow, not apprehend. This did little to reassure her. I dislike disappointing Kate. She rarely disappoints me, so this seems an unfair exchange. What is a bailiff to do when duty to his lord conflicts with his wife's wishes? What compromise is possible?

The holy man reported that the man he saw departing Bampton had been seen early in the night, before the moon rose to illuminate the road. No man appeared Saturday evening, although 'tis possible he may have crept past my hiding place while I drowsed. But I think not.

Sunday was forty days since Gilbert's birth. Kate departed Galen House after mass, wearing a veil and carrying a lighted candle. Father Thomas met her at the porch, and

Kate knelt whilst the priest sprinkled holy water on her from the newly filled font. Father Thomas then led Kate and her attendants to the altar, where she offered the candle, a penny, and Gilbert's chrism cloth to the priest.

When Kate's churching was concluded, it was my obligation, as the proud father, to provide a feast for the god's sibs who had attended Kate at Gilbert's birth. Adela had roasted three capons and I provided wheaten loaves and honeyed butter.

Sunday night was quiet, and both nights when I gave up the watch and returned to Galen House it was with aching joints that I did so. I am becoming too old to sit upon dewy ground in the night.

But Monday night my vigil was rewarded. A sliver of new moon provided little light, so I heard, more than saw, movement as some man walked quietly past my hiding place at the intersection of Broad Street and Laundels Lane.

I followed, close enough that I occasionally glimpsed or heard my quarry, but distant enough that I was not detected. The fellow had walked cautiously past my hiding place, but half a mile beyond Laundels Lane, beyond any village houses, he quickened his pace and made small effort to proceed on his way undetected.

Until he came to Lew. Then he slowed again and kept close to the verge, where he might blend with the summer verdure.

And then he disappeared. One moment he was thirty or so paces before me, the next he had vanished. As if I had blinked my eyes and caused the fellow to melt away.

I stopped, not wishing to come upon the man without warning; worried that he might have discovered my pursuit and lay in wait to crease my skull with a barrel stave or some other inflexible object. So I also sought the verge, and stood motionless. For several minutes I heard nothing, no furtive footsteps; nor did I see anything.

I was about to give up the chase and creep off toward Bampton when a faint, unidentifiable sound came to my ears. I listened intently and heard it again. Louder this time. Loud enough that I could identify the sound and the direction from whence it came.

'Twas the giggle of a lass, coming from a small barn which stood blackly a few paces from the road. Had I followed a man from Bampton to a tryst with a lass of Lew? Was he not the holy water thief? Would he eventually continue on to Witney? The holy man had not seen the fellow carry a skin or ewer; nor had I. How, then, could he carry holy water to Witney?

I had no desire to overhear an assignation. But I did wonder who of Bampton had periodically traveled to meet a lass of Lew. The lass had better look to her future. Sir Thomas, Lord of Lew, might charge her and her parents for lierwite and childwite.

I returned to Bampton and resumed my hiding place at Laundels Lane. An hour later my somnolence was interrupted. 'Twas the man I had followed to Lew, of this I was sure, now returning to Bampton. I thought to warn him of the peril he could bring upon his inamorata, but decided such a confrontation could wait until I had followed him to his home.

The man, now that he had entered the town, crept cautiously from shadow to shadow. He was not easy to follow. He traveled Broad Street, crossed Shill Brook, then entered the Weald. At Stephen Parkin's house he pushed open the unbarred door and entered. 'Twas Adela's brother!

Did Adela know of her brother's tenebrous travel? Even if she did not, she might repeat conversations between me and Kate which would tell her brother of my thoughts and intentions. Did he use that information for his own purposes, or share it with others? Others who might seek holy water, even if he did not.

And why was the door to Stephen Parkin's home unbarred? Did the man's parents know of his night-time rambles? Or might he have devised a way to lift the bar, silently, whilst his elderly parents snored peacefully in their bed?

Did the lad occasionally travel beyond Lew? To Witney? If so, mayhap two men took holy water from St. Beornwald's font. This seemed unlikely, but unlikely does not mean impossible.

What of the stolen holy water's use? Did two thieves provide holy water to one man, or did Adela's brother and the nocturnal visitor the holy man saw leaving St. Beornwald's have some personal use for the holy water? If so, what could it be? Nay, 'twas my opinion that a third party eventually acquired the holy water for some purpose of which I was ignorant.

I might have been ignorant of the use to which the holy water was put, but John Tey was not. Of this I was sure.

It was time to confront Roger Parkin. I told Adela that I wished to speak to her brother – he should attend me at Galen House when he'd finished his labor for the day. As the lad was a resident of the Weald, he was the Bishop of Exeter's tenant and I could not compel his obedience. But I could make life unpleasant for uncooperative folk of the Weald, which all knew. I expected Roger to appear after supper. He did.

I answered the rapping upon Galen House door and found Roger, cap in hand, with a worried expression on his face. He tugged a forelock but did not speak. Like the holy man, he waited for me to initiate the conversation.

What I had to say – some of it – was not for Bessie's ears. "Walk with me," I said, and led Roger to the church. The evening Angelus was past. We could converse in the porch unseen and unheard.

"You were upon the road late last night," I began. Roger could not have been more stunned than if I had swatted him across the cheek with a rotted stockfish. "What was the attraction in Lew which drew you there past midnight?" This was a rhetorical question. Unless my ears had deceived me, I knew full well what enticed the lad to walk the road on a dark night.

Roger stammered something about my being mistaken whilst he collected his thoughts. Being nowhere near as keen as Adela, gathering his meager thoughts took little time.

"Do not trouble yourself to deny it," I said. "I followed you home."

The lad's countenance fell when he learned this, and realized that whatever alibi he considered would be of no avail.

"'Twas a foolish question," I said. "I know why you traveled to Lew. What is the lass's name?"

Roger did not immediately answer, but glanced about the porch as if he might find some way to escape my probing into his life. "Maggie ... Margarite," he finally said.

"Do you intend to ask for her hand?"

"Can't," he muttered.

"Why so?"

"Sir Thomas won't allow it."

Lew, like most places in the realm, has been much reduced as plague has come again and again. The Lord of Lew would not want a fecund lass to wed a man from some other village. He would demand she choose a suitor from Lew, so as to enlarge his manor with her offspring. And Roger would not be welcome in Lew, having no coin and being the son of a poor cotter eking out a living as a tenant of the Bishop of Exeter.

"How did you come to meet a maid of Lew?"

"Accident, like. Seen 'er plantin' dredge."

Roger is a handsome lad, broad-shouldered. I suppose a pert lass might be as interested in him as he in her. Only after a conversation or two would a maid learn that his wit is not so broad as his shoulders. Would that make any difference to a lass who could see better than she could think?

"You saw her at work in her father's field? What took you to Lew?"

Another silence followed this question. I waited. My patience was not rewarded. Roger did not answer, and when I pressed him on the matter his only reply was, "Can't say."

"Can't, or won't?" I said.

Again, no reply.

"The roads are not safe," I said. "If you saw Maggie at work in one of her father's strips you must have walked the road in the day. What caused you to risk such travel?"

"Hah!" the lad replied. "No danger for such as me, what wears tattered chauces an' me father's frayed cotehardie. No thief would reckon I'd 'ave anythin' worth stealin'."

I didn't add, but could have, that a glance at Roger's beefy shoulders under the frayed cotehardie might convince a robber to seek a less formidable, as well as more lucrative, victim.

Did Roger walk to Lew for some purpose, or did he walk past Lew? To Witney, mayhap? There was a man, or men, who walked from Bampton to Witney in the night. They did so to collect St. Beornwald's holy water. Roger would not be one who would do such a thing. Would he? And for what purpose?

Roger remained silent, staring at his feet, which were bare, it being summer and leather expensive. For what purpose? The poll tax? Roger and Adela had a younger sister. The family would owe twenty pence to the king. The new king. How much could the sale of holy water bring?

Did Roger smite Father Robert that night in the church and leave him near dead? I could not believe it so. The lad, what little I knew of him, seemed a peaceable sort. Was he in league with some other? A man of Witney? The barrel stave used against Father Robert came from the cast-offs of the Witney cooper. I was convinced of this. Roger would not have needed to travel to Witney to find a cudgel stout enough to drop Father Robert to the church tiles. A brief stroll through Lord Gilbert's forest would have provided what he sought.

If Roger consorted with some man of Witney to steal holy water from St. Beornwald's font, and if John Tey was somehow involved in the theft, then it was likely to be the man of Witney who disposed of the holy water. Roger Parkin had not traveled to Oxford ever in his life – of this I felt certain.

Was all this for the purpose of black arts, and if so did Roger Parkin know the use for which purloined holy water was destined? He seemed a devout lad, no less interested in preparing for the next life than most lads of his age. Thoughts of the gates of pearl do not generally become common until arthritic joints propel such maunderings into a man's mind. Would Roger risk his soul for enough coins to pay his family's poll tax? A man wealthy enough to hire priests and monks to pray him out of purgatory would be prosperous enough to pay the tax. A man too poor to pay the poll tax would be too destitute to pay priests and monks to pray him from purgatory. If there is such a place. I must be careful of what I write. On the other hand, no bishop is likely to read this account.

"You traveled past Lew for a purpose," I tried again. "What was it?"

Still Roger remained silent. He might be dull, but he had enough wit to understand that silence seldom gets a man into trouble. Seldom, but occasionally. A man who will not speak allows his questioner to assume answers which may be correct or may be in error. If the inquisitor then acts upon a mistaken assumption, the consequences for the mute fellow may not be as he hoped.

But a man unjustly charged with a felony will oft name the guilty – if he knows the man – to save his own skin. "Roger," I said, "you leave me no choice but to charge you with the theft of holy water from the font of St. Beornwald's Church and the wounding of Father Robert when he sought to stop the crime."

"N-nay," Roger stammered. "I'd not do such a thing."

"If not you, who? Some man from Witney with whom you are in league? Name him and 'twill go easier for you."

"I cannot."

"Have you been threatened? What more can some schemer do to you than the Bishop of Exeter?"

Roger was not of my bailiwick, and the theft of holy water was a crime against the Church, not Lord Gilbert – although Lord Gilbert was certainly unhappy about what had happened in his parish church. I must turn Roger over to Father Thomas. No castle dungeon for him. How and where the priest could secure his prisoner I did not know. That was his problem.

Was Roger guilty as I had charged him? Mayhap. If not, he had only to name the man who had conspired with him to remove the threat to his future. Holy Mother Church hangs no man, but if the Bishop of Exeter turns a rogue over to the Sheriff of Oxford with the suggestion that a scaffold might be in order, the sheriff is likely to comply.

Roger did not know this. His imagination, I believe, did not encompass events more than a day or two into the future. That a hempen rope could be a prospect had not entered his mind. Until I planted the suggestion. The lad stiffened as the thought of entertaining the folk of Oxford by dangling at the end of a rope came to him. Such an image will wonderfully concentrate a man's mind.

"Told me 'twas for a good purpose," Roger said.

"What was? And who told you?"

Silence. Then, reluctantly, he spoke a name: "John."

"John who?" Several men of that name reside in Bampton and the Weald.

"John Faceby."

The name was unknown to me. "Where does the man reside?"

"Witney."

"And what good purpose might he achieve in employing holy water? Was it not for magic and the black arts that the water was required?"

"Nay. John said 'twas needful for folk what was took ill, plague an' such."

"And he paid you to take holy water from St. Beornwald's font? When did you do so?"

"Nay. I never took no holy water."

"But the man paid you for some service, did he not?"

Another extended silence. "Aye," Roger said softly.

"What benefit did you offer, was it not stolen holy water?"

"Information."

"About the font? When it was empty? When it was refilled?"

"Aye."

"And what else?"

Roger might not have answered this question and I would have been none the wiser, but I believe the thought of a noose lingered at the back of his mind. "Information."

"So you said. What more than information about the font could he want?"

"Wanted to know of your business."

"My business? You mean my investigation into the thefts of holy water?"

"Aye."

"What could you tell him? You are not privy to my thoughts." As I said this, I knew who was, and how Roger might have discovered my plans. Adela! When I traveled to Oxford to seek the locksmith, Tey usually knew I was coming. When the clerks of St. Beornwald's returned to Bampton with a new lock, men had accosted them and seized the lock. Did the felons learn from John Tey of the clerks' return with a new lock, or did they have another source of information?

Did Adela know of her brother's part in the theft of holy water? I could not believe it so. But did she, when under her parents' roof, speak of matters she had heard about at Galen House? Matters which Roger would overhear? That I could believe.

And who had peered at me from the scrub when Uctred and I splashed across the Thames at Swinford? Roger? If so, what was his intent? Had some scoundrel hired him to interfere with my possession of the new lock and its journey to Bampton?

I had spoken to Kate of my suspicion that John Tey made a second key, which was now in the possession of some scoundrel. Was Adela present when I said this? Probably.

Chapter 12

I had learned as much as I thought possible from Roger, and if there was more I required of him I knew where to find him. I dismissed the lad and watched as he hurried under the lychgate and toward the Weald.

If Roger was to be believed, the stolen holy water was not being employed in black arts, but rather to offer men a cure for their afflictions. At a price. Coins were changing hands. Someone was paying two locksmiths. A man named John Faceby was paying Roger Parkin. Folk needed coins to pay their poll tax, which in Bampton would be required of them in a few more months. Could I blame Roger for trying to find a way to assist his parents in collecting the funds required of them?

Men who purchased holy water to cure their ills would know they were committing an offense. If they knew they were buying holy water. But why spend coins for unsanctified water? Certainly they knew what they were getting. How did they use the holy water? Did they drink it? Bathe a swelling bubo with the stuff? Did some heretical physician supply the holy water and, for a fee, advise in its use?

Such thoughts occupied my mind as I departed the porch and sought my home. It was nearly dark. Kate had put John and Bessie to bed, and was awaiting my return to bar the door. I'm sure she was also curious about my reason for speaking privily to Roger Parkin.

I told her of Roger's part in informing the holy water thief of the state of St. Beornwald's font. And of Adela's loose tongue.

"You believe Adela knows of her brother's act?" Kate said. "If so, I will immediately dismiss her."

"Nay. Servants do like to prattle of their employers' business. If we discover that she knew of his betrayal it will then be time enough to sack her."

"There was another who took holy water from the font," Kate reminded me. "You and Uctred followed him to the east, you said, and just beyond St. Andrew's Chapel he had a beast waiting."

"Aye. We heard the hoofbeats as he rode away, but did not see the man."

Was Roger feeding information to a second man, or was John Faceby in league with another? If I went to Witney, found John Faceby, and pressed him, would he tell me of an accomplice? If he had one.

Occasionally partners in crime will turn on each other if doing so might mitigate their punishment. I had no way of discovering the horseman who had evidently acquired a key to St. Beornwald's font, unless he was a collaborator with Faceby. 'Twas time to visit Witney again, disagreeable as the journey might be.

Uctred was not surprised on Wednesday morning when I asked him to accompany me to Witney. He was becoming accustomed to my peripatetic behavior, and there was little of interest happening at the castle. Which thought caused me to reflect on Lord Gilbert's journey to London. King Edward would be buried in Westminster Abbey, amongst his ancestors, and his grandson crowned in the same edifice. Had either of these events happened yet, I wondered? The old king's funeral would take place before the coronation. Probably.

Uctred got two aged palfreys ready, and we arrived in Witney shortly after the third hour, the old palfreys keeping a decent pace and seeming to enjoy their release from the stables.

John Faceby was unknown to me, but would be known to the rector of St. Mary's Church. I went directly there. The priest greeted me as I entered the porch, and before I could speak he offered the news that, since securing his font key in the rectory, no more holy water had been taken from the font.

"I am pleased to hear it," I said, "but I seek you on another matter. Is there a man named Faceby in your parish?"

"Aye. John."

"Before you moved your font key to your rectory, did John Faceby ever enter the sacristy?"

"Not so far as I know. You suspect him of taking the holy water?"

"Is he, in your opinion, a trustworthy man?"

"Aye. A simple fellow, is John."

"Prosperous?"

"Not poor. He has enough of this world's goods that folk have asked him and Milicent to stand as godparents. Not two months past they became godparents to Henry and Amabil's babe."

"When they did so, would John have seen you enter the sacristy and return with the key to the font?"

The priest furrowed his brow in an attempt to remember. "I don't believe so," he finally said. "'Tis my practice to have all in readiness when a babe is to be baptized. I would have unlocked the font before the godparents brought the babe to the church."

My theory was demolished. I thought John Faceby might have had some reason to enter the sacristy, or to see the rector enter and return with the font key. Not so.

"Did the babe's father then offer a feast for the godparents and god's sibs and you?"

"Of course."

"Did you replace the font key *before* attending, or after?"

"Before. Why do you ask?"

"Could John Faceby have seen you enter the sacristy to replace the key as he departed the church?"

"He might have. 'Twas many weeks past. I cannot call events to remembrance. You think John may have made off with holy water when it went missing from St. Mary's Church?"

"There is reason to believe it so."

"Will you tell the reason?"

"A man of Bampton has confessed to providing John Faceby with information about the state of St. Beornwald's font – when it was empty and when it was newly filled."

"Has John traveled to Bampton for the purpose of taking holy water? What would he do with it?"

"'Tis my belief that he and at least one other scoundrel are selling the holy water in Oxford."

"For what purpose? Black arts?"

"So I thought, but I now believe 'tis being sold to folk who seek cures for their illnesses."

"But why do so? They could pay priests and monks to pray for their afflictions and light candles in their parish churches."

"So they could. But why do you dunk a babe three times into the font?"

"To drive out demons who would otherwise attempt to seize a babe's soul. Ah, I catch your drift. If holy water can drive demons from a babe, it might also drive away the demons who cause a man's illness."

"Just so," I agreed. "Where does John Faceby live?"

"On Moss Street. I will take you there."

Faceby's home backed against the Windrush river. This was convenient, as he was a dyer and could easily fill his vats. Across the street was Puck Lane and the cooper's shop. We found Faceby stirring a vat of wool and woad. His paddle and hands were stained a vivid blue. If the dyer was surprised to see his priest appear in company with a stranger, he hid it well.

"Father Simon, how may I serve you?" he said, laying his paddle aside.

"Here is Sir Hugh de Singleton," the priest said. "Bailiff to Lord Gilbert Talbot at Bampton, come to Witney to ask information of you."

"I know nothing of matters in Bampton," Faceby said.

"Hmm. There is a man of Bampton – the Weald, actually – who knows a good deal about matters here in Witney. His name is Roger Parkin."

The dyer took an involuntary step back when he heard Roger's name, but quickly gathered his wits. "Don't know a man of that name," he said.

"He is the son of a poor cotter, who needs coins to pay the poll tax. To acquire what his family needs he has sold you information."

"What information of Bampton do I need?"

"Information as to when the font of St. Beornwald's Church is newly filled, so you may help yourself to the holy water."

"Bah! The man lies who says I did so."

161

"And across the street is the cooper's shop, where you collected a split stave and used it to break the head of a priest of St. Beornwald's Church, who interfered with your thievery. A dyer can have no legitimate use for holy water. What did you do with the water you stole? Sell it? Where?"

Faceby looked from me to the priest to his vat, as if rummaging through his brain for some falsehood I might find believable. Good luck with that. Even when I hear truth I am inclined to doubt it. I have been a bailiff too long.

Evidently, Faceby's search was a failure. He decided to tell the truth, which I later took pains to verify. "Sold it in Oxford," he muttered.

"To whom?"

"An herbalist."

"On St. Mildred's Street?"

"Aye."

I began to see the pattern. The herbalist sold holy water to physicians, who then charged their patients for the stuff. To keep a supply flowing, the locksmiths of Oxford were paid to not provide locks for baptismal fonts. Had holy water been drawn from fonts in other churches, other towns, where mayhap the loss had not been discovered? I thought this likely.

I had found one holy water thief, the one who assailed Father Robert, but there was another: he who had mounted a horse just east of St. Andrew's Chapel. And Faceby had assaulted Father Robert. He must pay the penalty for this offense. Who would decide what that should be? The Bishop of Exeter? Lord Gilbert?

There was a second key to St. Beornwald's font in some man's hands. Probably the fellow who had mounted a horse to the east of St. Andrew's Chapel and ridden east toward Oxford. The herbalist who sold purloined holy water had two suppliers, and one of these possessed John Tey's second key.

The rector said, "John has taken holy water from both the Church of St. Mary and the Church of St. Beornwald. Which shall have jurisdiction and determine his punishment?"

"Theft of holy water is an offense against the Church. The Bishop of Exeter, when he learns of the felonies, will claim authority," I said.

"And welcome to it."

"Will you send him a letter telling of this man's villainies, or should I tell the vicars of St. Beornwald's Church to do so?"

"The roads are not safe," Father Simon said. "Mayhap two letters should be sent, so if one goes astray the other will reach the bishop."

"Aye. No clerk or servant will be pleased with the task. As you say, roads are not safe, and the coronation of a boy king will not make them safer."

Faceby looked from me to Father Simon as we discussed his future, then spoke. "What punishment will the bishop order?"

"Who can say?" the rector replied. "Perhaps a fine."

A bishop's decisions are not predictable. His judgment might depend upon his mood – whether or not his cook's dinner pleased him that day, or his mistress has been ill-tempered of late.

"There is another punishment you should dread," I said. "The bishop will learn that you wounded a priest who interfered with your theft of holy water. Holy Church slays no man, but if the bishop decides to place your fate in the hands of the Sheriff of Oxford, you may entertain the burghers of the town with the sheriff's dance."

I saw Faceby blanche when the import of my words struck home. Would the bishop exact such a penalty? This might depend on Father Robert's recovery, or his desire for either vengeance or mercy. Father Robert, I thought, would choose mercy. I said this to Faceby, but warned him that he should not rely upon my opinion of another man's views.

I had learned much this day, some of which I had suspected, much I had not. Uctred and I left Faceby and Father Simon frowning at each other and retraced our steps to the rectory, where we had left our palfreys. In little more than an hour we entered Bampton, where I dismounted at Galen House and sent Uctred to the castle with the palfreys.

My dinner was late and grown cold, but as 'twas a fast day the loss was not great. A pea and bean pottage, flavored with leeks and onions, awaited me.

Kate was eager to learn of my travel to Witney, but when she asked for a report I cast a glance toward Adela from the corner of my eye and she changed the subject. Gilbert, she said, suffered from a colic. Was there any herb which might soothe his discomfort? I knew of none, and was reluctant to experiment with remedies I might give to adults, having no knowledge of their effect on a babe.

When I had consumed my fill of the green-complected dinner, I decided to visit Father Robert. I wished to learn of his convalescence and tell him his assailant was now known. The plaster I had daubed over his broken skull could now be removed. For this he would be grateful, as he would henceforth be able to scratch his pate when he had an itch. But I must warn him to be gentle. Nothing vigorous for a few more weeks. Perhaps by Lammastide he would no longer be concerned about his skull. And by then he'd have some hair to soften any blow – so long as the whack was not delivered with a barrel stave.

Piers answered my knock on Father Robert's vicarage door. "Ah, you have come to examine Father Robert," he guessed.

"Indeed. How does he?"

"Come and see," he said, and led me to the small hall.

I found Father Robert sitting upon a bench before a desk. The desk had been drawn before a glass window, and a Bible lay open to the summer sun.

"Ah, Sir Hugh . . . you are well met," he said and began to rise.

"Nay," I said. "Remain seated."

"Why, when I can rise?" Then, to prove this ability, he stood. Slowly, to be sure, and favoring his left leg, but rise he did.

"A miracle, is it not?" the priest said. "I have been reading from the ninth chapter of the book of the Acts of the Apostles, where St. Peter healed Aeneas, who had been unable to leave his bed for eight years. You are like St. Peter."

"Nay," I protested. "I work no miracles."

"Not so. Without your skill I would be as confined to my bed as Aeneas. If I lived at all. Is not your training and skill a miracle?"

The plaster about Father Robert's head was cracked and tattered. I tried to lift it whole, but it was fixed in some places to his newly grown hair, and in other places so broken that it came away from his skull in pieces. Hair had grown back to cover the stitches I had made to close the wound over the broken fragment of skull. I dislike leaving sutures for so long before they are removed, but if the plaster were to remain in place this could not be helped.

I told the priest that removing the stitches would cause some discomfort – something between a prick and a sting – then drew from my instruments pouch a scalpel and tweezers. Slicing through the silk was easy, but pulling the threads from Father Robert's scalp took some tugging. The silk had become one with the skin, and resisted removal. The ache must have been considerable, but the priest bore it well.

A few dots of blood appeared where the sutures had penetrated the scalp. These I blotted away with a scrap of linen, and in the process gently pressed the place on his head where I had replaced the bone fragment. It seemed sturdy enough.

Father Robert sensed what I was doing and asked if I was pleased with the way his fractured skull had knit.

"Aye, but you must take care until Lammastide, or even after, that you do not receive another such blow."

"You need not be concerned about that," he laughed. "I will be cautious in dealing with men with clubs."

"Speaking of such men," I said, "I have found the man who broke your head."

"Indeed? Is he of Bampton, or the Weald?"

"Neither. His name is John Faceby. A dyer of Witney."

"He came to Bampton to take holy water from our font?"

"Aye. He has admitted so."

"What was his purpose? Black arts?"

"Nay. He sold holy water from the Church of St. Beornwald and also the Church of St. Mary the Virgin in Witney to an herbalist in Oxford, who then sold it to physicians for use in treating patients with illnesses which resist cures."

"Plague?"

"Aye. And others."

"Then our troubles are past and St. Beornwald's font will now be secure."

"I fear not."

"Why so?"

I told Father Robert of the possible second key to St. Beornwald's font and the mysterious nocturnal visitor to the church who, somewhere to the east of St. Andrew's Chapel, had found a horse and ridden off toward Oxford.

"Might the locksmith be innocent of making a second key?" Father Robert asked. "I have heard tell of making an impression of a key in wet clay, then pouring molten bronze into the mold to reproduce a key."

"Such a thing can be done, but to make a second key to fit the lock of St. Beornwald's font the forger would have to get the first key from Father Thomas."

"Oh . . . aye. So a second key would surely be the locksmith's doing, then?"

"So I believe."

But how to prove it? Only by catching the second holy water thief and extracting from him an accusation against John Tey. How could that be done? I had squandered too much time setting traps and hiding in the dark verge of a wood to believe it worthwhile to do so again. Well, nay. The time had not been wholly wasted. I had caught Roger Parkin, and through him discovered John Faceby.

The second holy water thief had ridden a horse to escape pursuit. A pursuit of which he was likely unaware. Was this his own beast? Few folk of Oxford can afford to keep a horse. Those who can do not need to sell stolen holy water to make ends meet. Or to pay their poll tax.

So where would a holy water thief acquire a beast? Probably from an inn. Would it be possible to discover the inn? And would a stable boy remember the man who took a horse one day, kept it overnight, and returned it the next day? *Probably* the next day.

How much could such a man profit if the gain from selling holy water was reduced by the cost of hiring a horse? Mayhap more coins changed hands in payment for holy water than I suspected. And men had already been hired to seize a new lock as the clerks returned from Oxford when the mystery of missing holy water was just beginning.

How much would a man be willing to pay for a possible cure if he saw the gates of pearl in his near future? Would he pay what coin he had to escape death awhile longer, or save his wealth and give it to a priest or monk to pray him sooner from purgatory?

No man can escape death. It comes for every man. Which is no reason to hasten its approach. Or fear it, if a man's faith is whole.

I bade Father Robert good day and set out for the castle. Uctred and I were going to visit those inns of Oxford which possessed stables. And I would not speak of the journey before Adela. Or Bessie and John.

Life at Bampton Castle while Lord Gilbert was away had settled into a comfortable routine. So when I told Uctred that he must again accompany me to Oxford on Thursday he did not seem overjoyed. No doubt the prospect of placing his bony posterior in a saddle for several hours was partly the cause of his reluctance.

I intended to depart Bampton before dawn, so few men would be up and about to see us depart the town.

I gave Uctred instructions that he was to prepare two palfreys himself, without telling the marshalsea what he was about. I was determined that we would arrive in Oxford before any man of Bampton or the Weald knew we were away.

The castle porter would have to raise the portcullis and lower the drawbridge so that Uctred could lead the palfreys from the castle. There was no helping that. But I thought it probable that after Uctred and the palfreys were away, the porter would raise the drawbridge, lower the portcullis, and return to his bed until dawn.

As before, the old palfreys we rode tired and slowed when we reached Swinford. But due to our early start we reached Oxford whilst most men were yet rubbing the sleep from their eyes.

The stable boy at the Fox and Hounds recognized us, and for four pence promised to care for and feed our beasts for the day. And no, the inn did not own horses which could be hired. The Green Dragon, a competitor, did, however.

It had been ten days since a man had entered St. Beornwald's Church in the night, helped himself to holy water, then to the east of St. Andrew's Chapel mounted a horse and disappeared into the night. Would a stable boy remember a rider who had hired a horse ten days past? Mayhap, if the fellow was a regular customer. But why would he be? Did he have another use for a horse? A need to travel to other places? To Witney, where he might collect holy water from John Faceby? The dyer said that he sold holy water to an herbalist in Oxford, but did he mean he took it there himself? Or did an intermediary call for the Witney holy water, pay Faceby, and deliver it to Oxford? I had not had the wit to ask the dyer, when I confronted him, how the holy water was moved to Oxford.

John Tey would not yet know I was in Oxford. Roger Parkin knew nothing of my whereabouts, although Adela would know when she arrived at Galen House that I was absent. When she returned to her home in the Weald she might speak of it, but by then I hoped my business in Oxford would be completed and I would be on my way home. I would seek a horseman first, then confront the locksmith with evidence he could not refute. So I thought.

The Green Dragon did indeed have horses for hire, and in fact one of these beasts was away when Uctred and I arrived at the establishment. But before this engagement no horse had been hired since Whitsuntide, long before some man had ridden away from Bampton with stolen holy water. The stable boy at the Green Dragon knew of no other inn where a man might hire a horse. There were in Oxford, he said, several stables where wealthier burghers kept a horse, but so far as he knew none of these offered horses for hire.

My excellent idea had come to nothing. But the journey might not come to nothing. I could yet surprise John Tey, although if he lied about making a second key I could not prove otherwise. Perhaps his behavior might change if he knew that I suspected his chicanery.

And it was time to confront the herbalist. He'd had a vat on a shelf when I earlier visited the place which I thought probably contained a potion for clysters. I knew of no other herbalist on St. Mildred's Street, so Tey's neighbor was likely the recipient of Faceby's holy water, and of the unknown tenebrous rider's as well.

Our route to St. Mildred's Street took us past the Fox and Hounds. It had been several hours since I consumed a loaf and a cup of ale for an early meal, so Uctred and I shared a roasted capon at the inn. I paid little attention to the other customers in the place, being more interested in my meal. But Uctred did.

"Look there," he said sharply, pointing past the entrance to the inn. "Ain't that the locksmith?"

It was. Tey's back was to us, but he turned to sidestep another – the street was crowded – and I recognized the fellow.

"He come from that alley," Uctred said.

'Twas nearly the third hour. Time for most burghers to open their shops. The locksmith did seem to hurry on his way, and his path would take him to St. Mildred's Street and his shop.

We made our way to the alley from whence Uctred had seen Tey appear, and out of curiosity I glanced down the shadowy passageway. I saw a lad of perhaps fifteen years pushing a small handcart. Piled on it was dung and straw. The lad had been mucking out a stable, and was now disposing of the manure. Into the Cherwell, no doubt.

We waited where the alley joined the street, and when the lad came near I produced from my purse a ha'penny, held it before him, and said, "A moment of your time."

The lad peered greedily at the coin and released the handles of his cart.

"Is there a stable behind the Fox and Hounds?" I asked.
"Aye."

"Does a man named John Tey keep a horse there?"
"Aye."

"For how long has he done so?"

The lad scratched his greasy hair and said, "'Bout Whitsuntide; mayhap a fortnight after."

I thanked the lad for the information and gave him the coin. I now thought I knew who the midnight rider east of St. Andrew's Chapel had been, and how John Tey could afford a horse. I was continually learning more about the profit possible in selling holy water.

But how did the locksmith discover when St. Beornwald's font was resupplied? Roger Parkin had provided that information to John Faceby. Had Roger also told Tey? If so, when? I doubted that Roger had ever traveled to Oxford, and Tey would have no reason to assume Roger knew anything about St. Beornwald's font and try to pry the knowledge from him. Likely the locksmith did not even know that Roger existed.

'Twas time to accost John Tey and confront the fellow with what I knew of his business.

We arrived at St. Mildred's Street as the locksmith raised his shutters. The herbalist and glover were already open for custom. Tey's back was turned as Uctred and I approached, so he did not know who had entered his shop. When he turned, his mouth dropped open.

"You have failed to greet me," I said. "Most shopkeepers will ask, 'How may I serve you?' when a customer enters his shop. But you already know how you may serve me. I will have the second key you made for the font lock for the Church of St. Beornwald in Bampton."

Tey gathered his wits quickly whilst stammering a denial. "S-second key?" he said. "I charged the vicars for but one key."

"Indeed. What they paid for and what you produced were two different things. Some man possessing a key to the font of St. Beornwald's Church has used it to take holy water. That man was seen departing the church in the night, and a short way east of Bampton he mounted a horse and set off for Oxford. You own a horse, as I have discovered."

"Many folk own a beast," Tey protested.

"You did not 'til a fortnight or so after Whitsuntide. You must have acquired a heavier purse about then. From the sale of multiple locks, I'd guess, and then the holy water. You saw that the profit from selling holy water could be greater than the gain from selling locks."

The locksmith did not protest the accuracy of my accusation. He knew, I believe, that he had been caught out, and perhaps thought I knew more about his felonies than I actually did. For some of my accusation was conjecture based upon logic and experience.

"Now," I said, "we will go next door and see what the herbalist has to say."

Tey glanced to his shop door and I thought for a moment that he intended to run. He was not a young man. Did he believe he could show his heels to me? I am not so swift as I once was, Kate's cookery being to blame, but I could surely chase down John Tey. As it happened, I would soon have opportunity to test the accuracy of that assumption.

I led Tey to the herbalist's shop while Uctred followed. The rotund herbalist looked up from crushing hemp seeds, set his mortar and pestle aside, and asked how he could serve me, as any polite burgher would. He was clearly puzzled by the locksmith's appearance with me, but would not allow his confusion to interfere with business.

"The small barrel which sits on yon shelf," I said. "I wish to inspect its contents."

"Uh . . . 'tis empty at the moment."

"Then I will find no reason to seek a serjeant to consider the barrel."

At the mention of a sheriff's man the herbalist blanched, color draining from his plump cheeks like breath from

Kate's mirror. I knew not what Sheriff de Elmerugg paid the king for the post, but to earn a return on investment a sheriff must levy fines upon burgers who violate the city's ordinances. Is there an Oxford statute against stealing and selling holy water? If not, a resourceful sheriff could invent some regulation forbidding the practice. The penalty, I felt sure, would be substantial. So did the herbalist.

Sheriff de Elmerugg had not returned from London, and the funeral and coronation, as all Oxford knew. I suspect the herbalist decided that feigned cooperation before the sheriff returned would be less costly than forced cooperation when de Elmerugg was back within Oxford Castle.

The herbalist reluctantly turned to the small barrel and lifted it from the shelf. He strained to do so. It was clear that the barrel was not empty.

"Ah," he exclaimed. "I forgot. I filled it yesterday."

"With what?" I said.

"Uh . . . a theriac . . . of my own devising."

"What is the purpose of this potion?"

"'Twill cure all manner of ailments," the herbalist claimed.

"Such as?"

"Uh . . . the pox, stones in the bladder, plague, toothache."

"Hmm, a wondrous concoction. What is in it?"

"I tell no man. I do not want my formula stolen."

"Understandable." I then lifted the lid and peered into the barrel. It contained perhaps four or five gallons of water. No herbs or powders sullied its purity. "There is nothing but water," I said.

"I . . . uh . . . have not yet added the ingredients."

"I have heard it said that a theriac must be aged for some months, even years, before it is potent," I said.

"My formula is not like others," the herbalist claimed with returning confidence.

"And the water," I said. "Is it pure? I saw a lad earlier today who had just mucked out a stable. He was, last I saw, pushing his cart toward the Cherwell. Is that the source of this water? Or the Thames?"

"Oh, nay. This water comes from the Windrush."

"The river which flows through Witney?"

"Aye. The same. And the water is drawn from the stream before the current enters the town, so none of the offal from the place is found in it."

"What of the refuse from Burford?" I said. "That town is upstream from Witney. And are you sure of that water's source? Did you collect the water yourself?"

"Uh, nay. A man of Witney draws the water for me."

"You trust John Faceby?"

The herbalist grasped the table to keep himself upright, else I believe my mention of the dyer's name would have caused him to topple to the floor.

Faceby's name also brought a reaction from John Tey. He bolted for the door. I shouted to Uctred to remain with the herbalist, then ran after the locksmith.

Chapter 13

Oxford's streets were thick with burghers and scholars. Tey scurried between folk at their business, and I gave chase. 'Twas remarkable how swift the fellow was. Of course, if I were pursued by a man who could charge me with a misdemeanor before a bishop's court, I might find speed of which I was previously unaware.

Tey ran to Ship Street, and was near to St. Michael's at the Northgate before I caught him. The locksmith stumbled over a wayward cur. The hound produced a sharp yelp and Tey skidded to his knees. I pounced upon him and the chase was ended. The locksmith was red in the face and panting.

Our brief tussle brought disapproving scowls from passers-by, for which I cared little. These folk did not know me, and would not see me again, as I was now sure that the mystery of stolen holy water was solved and I would have no need to return to Oxford.

I hoisted Tey to his feet, grasped his collar with one hand, and placed the other hand on the hilt of my dagger. I had no desire to draw it against the man, but thought if he saw this it might have a salutary effect upon his behavior. It did. He walked submissively back to St. Mildred's Street.

The herbalist and Uctred stood facing each other, just as they were when I ran after John Tey. The herbalist knew that his stumpy legs could not propel his well-fed body away from the pursuit of even a bow-legged codger like Uctred.

A well-dressed man, garbed in a cotehardie of fine wool and parti-colored chauces, followed Tey and me through the door of the herbalist's shop. A perplexed frown wrinkled the man's brow. I saw, from the corner of my eye, the herbalist shake his head – so slightly I nearly missed the movement. He was looking at the newcomer as he did so. Here was a message delivered. The herbalist knew the query before he was asked. He had done business with this customer before.

What did the man want which the herbalist did not want to provide? Some palliative of which his supply was exhausted? Why not simply say so? Why the surreptitious communication? These questions flashed through my mind more rapidly than I can write of them. And the answer, also. Here was a physician, one of many who inhabit Oxford, ready to purchase a flask of holy water with which to treat a patient. A prosperous patient.

If holy water in a baptismal font can drive the devil from an infant and thus preserve his soul, and if Satan is sometimes responsible for the afflictions which trouble mankind, then the use of holy water to cure illness is logical. Did this physician's patients know of the source of their treatment? I doubted it. If they did, sooner or later one would let slip the information, especially if they were restored to health and friends asked of the medication which worked the cure.

The visitor turned on his heel and hurriedly departed the shop. What now? Must I resort to finger-wagging and fist-shaking to wring the truth from Tey and the herbalist? What good would such demonstrations do? I decided upon a simple declaration of the facts as I knew them, trusting that such a recitation would bring a halt to the theft and misuse of holy water.

"You have no theriac or special formula in that barrel," I said to the herbalist. "You have there holy water, taken from the fonts of churches in Bampton and Witney, and who knows what other churches.

"And you," I said to John Tey, "were paid to resist the manufacture of a new lock for the font of St. Beornwald's Church, and when a new lock was finally crafted you hired rogues to waylay the clerks of St. Beornwald's and take it back. When you could no longer keep a new lock from being fixed to St. Beornwald's font you made two keys, deciding to cut out a middleman and use the second key yourself to contrive to take the holy water. How much," I said to the herbalist, "did you pay Faceby and Tey for the holy water they provided?"

The herbalist looked to Tey, then said, "Two shillings to the gallon."

"And what did you charge the physicians and others who purchased it from you?"

He did not immediately reply, but finally said, "Six pence to the pint."

"Hah! Four shillings to the gallon. You doubled your cost. Of course, you had to pay Faceby and Tey for other expenses, I assume. The three scoundrels who accosted the clerks and took back the first lock had to be paid as well."

"Why do you beset me so?" the herbalist complained. "Holy water is used for many common practices. Folk sprinkle it upon a grave before 'tis dug to speed the dead past purgatory, and 'tis sprinkled upon the marriage bed to promote childbearing."

"Indeed," I agreed, "but in these and other cases it is employed by a priest who has taken holy orders, not some profane herbalist seeking profit. There is at least a gallon of holy water in yon barrel, mayhap two. It must not be disposed of in some sacrilegious manner. Send it to Bampton to refill the font at St. Beornwald's Church. I will tell the vicars to expect delivery anon.

"You," I addressed the locksmith, "have a horse. You can be in Bampton in little more than two hours, shortly after I and my man arrive there. See to the delivery of the holy water, and give the second font key to Father Thomas whilst you are about it."

"'Twas for the good of them what's taken ill," the herbalist said defensively. "A man what seeks a cure for his affliction should expect to pay him what works the cure."

"Explain that to the Bishop of Exeter, whose font in St. Beornwald's Church you despoiled. You paid the locksmith to absent himself when I came to St. Mildred's Street seeking him. I saw the note you left behind his shutter. No lock meant continued access to St. Beornwald's font. As for a man being willing to pay for a cure provided by the misuse of holy water, again explain that to the Bishop of Exeter."

The herbalist did not reply. I suspected a meeting with the Bishop of Exeter was an encounter he would prefer to avoid.

John Tey had known when I planned to visit Oxford, seek him, and obtain a new lock. How could he have known this? Adela was aware of my intentions. No doubt she spoke my purpose in her brother's presence. How much had Tey paid Roger for information? Enough to provide coins for the Parkin family poll tax? When parliament levied the poll tax, had they considered the hardship it would cause? And the thievery, as men sought the wealth of others to meet their obligations? Perhaps even the herbalist and John Tey saw the sale of holy water as a way to meet their debt to the king.

Uctred and I had departed Bampton before dawn. 'Twas now near the ninth hour. Days in July are long, so there was time to return to Bampton before darkness might bring thieves from the shadows.

Our beasts were well rested, which could not be said of Uctred and me. As the horses plodded past Eynsham Abbey I swayed in the saddle, and in occasional alert moments I saw Uctred do the same. Our progress beyond Eynsham was so slow I thought John Tey might catch us. He did not. Mayhap his horse was as old as the mounts Uctred and I rode.

Where Church View Street meets Bridge Street I dismounted, sent Uctred to the castle with the palfreys, and strode stiffly to Galen House. Perhaps I am too old to ride to Oxford and return in one day. One long day. No man likes to admit he can no longer perform the feats of his youth. But whether he admits it or not, the fact remains.

I stopped at Galen House just long enough to advise Kate that I had returned, then hurried to Father Thomas's vicarage. John Tey had not yet arrived, but the priest was delighted to learn that he would receive the holy water – enough to nearly fill the font – and the second key.

"You think the theft of holy water is not likely to happen again?" Father Thomas said.

"I am neither a prophet nor the son of a prophet," I replied. "But aye, I believe the scoundrels who traded in your holy water are found out and will do so no longer."

"Traded?"

"Aye. 'Twas a business, in part." I related to the priest what I had learned this day from the herbalist and locksmith.

"And the locksmith is even now on his way to Bampton?" Father Thomas smiled.

"So he was instructed. What may happen after he arrives is up to you and the bishop. The theft of holy water is beyond my bailiwick."

"Bishop Bokyngham will be informed straightaway. What of the man who smote Father Robert?"

"That also is the bishop's decision. For two hundred years, since the time of Becket, such matters have been the business of the Church."

"Just so," Father Thomas agreed. "By the way," he continued, "news came this morning that King Edward's funeral was Sunday last, his burial in Westminster, and Richard of Bordeaux is to be crowned a week from today, again at Westminster."

"A boy king. 'Woe to you, O land, when your king *is* a child,' so Solomon wrote. Of course, I do not necessarily trust the counsel of a man who had seven hundred wives and three hundred concubines," I said.

"A boy king," Father Thomas said, "who will not lack for advisors. We must hope they will all be simple men."

"Do not count on it," I replied.

"Sir Hugh, you have a suspicious nature."

"It comes with the job. And what does Holy Writ say about men's hearts?"

"They are deceitful and wicked."

"Just so. Unless the Lord Christ has worked in the man.

"We should go to the church," I continued. "The corrupt locksmith should arrive soon, and he will likely seek you at the church, not knowing of your vicarage."

"You trust the locksmith to do as he promised. I thought you trusted no man?"

181

"A man who sees some unpredictable punishment in his future if he does not do as required is likely to be trustworthy. At least in the matter before him."

The priest and I walked to St. Beornwald's Church and sat in the cool of the porch to await John Tey. I could barely keep my eyes open and was struggling to remain vertical when Father Thomas elbowed me in the ribs. "He comes," the priest said.

This announcement brought me awake and I peered past the entry. 'Twas as Father Thomas said. The locksmith had alighted at the lychgate and was tying his palfrey to it as I watched.

I took a few steps from the porch so Tey could see that I awaited him. The barrel from the herbalist's shop was secured behind his beast's saddle and he went to work loosening the bindings, paying me no heed, although he surely saw me awaiting him.

The barrel's weight was substantial and Tey struggled to raise it to his shoulder. When he did, he finally allowed his gaze to fall on me and Father Thomas, then stumbled to the porch. I might have offered to assist him, but it was his choice to see the holy water removed from St. Beornwald's font, so he could see to its return. Perhaps this was ungracious. I will ask the Lord Christ's forgiveness. Later.

Father Thomas led the way to the font, produced his key, and raised the lid. He motioned to the uncovered basin and the locksmith removed the bung, tilted the barrel, and filled the font. Nearly to overflowing.

When he was done, I took the barrel from him. "You'll not be needing this in the future," I said. I had no particular use for a small barrel, but thought with the passage of time I might find one. I did, but that is another tale.

Father Thomas closed and locked the font, and we set off for the door to the porch. Tey stood by the font, unmoving.

"Where am I to go?" he said. "The roads are not safe. 'Twill be dark before I can gain Oxford."

"Travel at night did not trouble you when you stole the holy water. Why should you worry now? What have you that men might steal?"

"My beast," he replied. "I must sell it so as to pay the poll tax."

"Ah . . . just so. Well, if you make haste you will arrive at Eynsham Abbey before dark. The guest master will find a place for you and your horse."

This reassurance animated the locksmith. He hurried to the lychgate, freed his horse, and soon disappeared down Church View Street.

I was curious about Father Robert's health, but more than that I was exhausted. I left Father Thomas at his vicarage, stumbled to Galen House, and managed to remain awake long enough to consume a supper of fraunt hemelle. 'Twas not yet dark when I sought my bed, but Morpheus claimed me only moments after my head dented the pillow.

I broke my fast on Friday with a maslin loaf and ale, then, after a suitable time had passed, I walked to Father Robert's vicarage and rapped upon the door.

Piers opened to me, and I was surprised to see Father Thomas already present. I suppose I should not have been. No doubt he had been eager to tell Father Robert of the resolution to the mystery of the stolen holy water.

I entered the vicarage and Father Robert stood as I did.

"Nay," I said. "Remain seated."

"I am no invalid," the priest said. "I am not so nimble as two months past, but I am stronger with each day which passes. The exercises you instructed Piers to work have produced a marvelous result. Perhaps, in a fortnight, I can discard this stick."

"Mayhap," I agreed.

This was not to be, and I had doubts when Father Robert spoke of it. But I held my tongue. It is of no benefit to a man to undermine his hope.

Was it the exercises I had instructed Piers to work with Father Robert, or would the priest have recovered so far as he had with no tugging and flexing at all? Who could know? And who could know how far along the road to recovery he would yet travel? Father Robert was younger than Lord Gilbert's verderer had been. Mayhap his youth would speed recovery. Age slows things.

"On another matter," I said, "the man of Witney who smote you, John Faceby, must be brought to justice. Shall he be turned over to Bishop Bokyngham, or would you have Lord Gilbert send him to the Sheriff of Oxford when they return from Richard of Bordeaux's coronation?"

"I would like to speak to the man before such a decision is made," Father Robert said.

"You cannot travel to him," Father Thomas said. "He must be brought here. What if he will not come?"

"Uctred and I," I said, "will convince him to do so."

"Today?" Father Robert asked.

"Certainly. I will go to the castle, seek Uctred and two – no, three – palfreys and be off for Witney. I'll have Faceby here by midday."

The dyer, I believe, expected another visit from me, but did not think it would include an invitation to visit Bampton. My tone of voice made clear to him that this visit was a command, not a request. And the third palfrey could mean but one thing: he was going to Bampton and would not be required to walk.

"You are to meet the priest you assaulted," I told him. "You will hear from him what your punishment may be, and who will administer it."

"'Twas not my intent to harm the priest. And had I known 'twas a priest I'd not have struck him. The church was dark. I would not abuse any man, but I needed to gain coins. I have four children and a wife. The poll tax will cost me two shillings; more than I earn in a fortnight."

Here was a lamentable tale which was being repeated with slight variations throughout the realm. How many men, I wonder, will do the sheriff's dance after being caught stealing so they may meet their obligations to the king? To a deceased king. Does a boy king require funds so he can raise an army to attack France and regain lost provinces? Nay. But his uncle may.

Faceby followed me to the street and mounted the palfrey reserved for him. He did so clumsily. Likely the back of a horse was unfamiliar to him.

Little more than an hour later we passed the tithe barn and stopped before Father Robert's vicarage. The dyer was as inept at dismounting as at mounting. Perhaps worry about his fate served to increase his awkwardness. He stumbled and nearly fell. He was as unsteady as Father Robert.

Piers heard us arrive and opened the vicarage door before I could rap on it. Father Ralph and Martyn had joined Father Thomas, Father Robert, and their clerks. The six clerics gazed at John Faceby with features empty of emotion. 'Twas impossible to gauge their sentiments. Until they spoke.

"Is this the scoundrel who broke Father Robert's head?" Father Ralph growled. "He should go to the castle dungeon until Lord Gilbert returns and can decide whether to send him to Bishop Bokyngham or Sheriff de Elmerugg."

"The sheriff and bishop are both in London," Father Robert said softly. "So rather than await their opinions, mayhap we here should resolve the matter."

"It was you who was attacked," Father Thomas said. "What is your view?"

The dyer looked to those who spoke of his future with his head on a swivel. His face was drawn with worry, as well it might be.

"We are to forgive those who despitefully use us," Father Robert said. "So the Lord Christ commanded."

"Aye," Father Thomas agreed. "But to forgive a wrong should not preclude punishment for sinful behavior, else dishonest men would go about doing evil and honest men would have no recourse. They would forgive those who plundered their homes 'til their possessions were looted, their wives and daughters ravished."

No one responded to Father Thomas's assertion. Which, I suppose, meant that we who heard the observation were in agreement. Even John Faceby was silent.

Father Robert finally broke the silence. "What you have said," he told Father Thomas, "makes sense. Indeed, to keep order in the realm it must be so. Nevertheless, I wish for this man to be released. To return to his wife and children. If forgiveness costs little, it is not worth much."

"You are sure of this?" I said.

"I have thought much about what should be done to the man who broke my head. I always come to the same conclusion. I forgive him and would see him go on his way."

"With a promise he will never do such a felony again," Father Ralph muttered. 'Twas clear he did not approve.

"I do so promise," Faceby said fervently.

"Then be off with you," Father Thomas said, "before Father Robert changes his mind."

The dyer turned and was out of the vicarage door in the blink of an eye. I watched him trot past the tithe barn, look over his shoulder, then disappear. He would waste no time, I thought, in returning to Witney.

All who remained in the vicarage also began to drift away. 'Twas time for dinner, although as this was a fast day the meal would not likely be memorable.

It was not. I consumed a bowl of peas pottage while I told Kate of Father Robert's decision.

"Mercy is a wonderful virtue in a priest," she said.

"Aye," I agreed. "'Tis unfortunate more bishops and archdeacons do not practice it."

Six days later, the sixteenth of July, Richard of Bordeaux, ten years of age, was crowned King of England. 'Twas a Thursday, for no coronation should happen upon a fast day. The feasting, Lord Gilbert told me later, was lavish, and wine flowed through the streets in red streams. Of course, neither I nor the other folk of Bampton knew of the coronation until Lord Gilbert and his retinue returned on Sunday, the nineteenth of July.

I knew at midday Sunday that Lord Gilbert had returned, for as I was pushing my bench back from a dinner of bouce jane I heard a manly thumping upon Galen House door. 'Twas Janyn and, like his father, when he knocked upon a door the rafters rattled.

"Good day, Janyn. Your presence at my door means that Lord Gilbert has completed his obligation to the past king, and to the new one."

"Aye. Streets between Whitehall an' Westminster was jammed with folk tryin' to catch a glimpse of the new king."

"Did you see him?"

"Aye. Frail-lookin' lad."

Why had Janyn appeared at Galen House? Was he sent from the castle to notify me of my employer's return? I asked him.

"Nay," he replied, and I saw a crimson flush expand upon his cheeks. "Come to see if Adela's done with her work this day."

"Wait here. I will speak to Lady Katherine and find out if she is." I turned to seek the kitchen, and as I did, my Kate appeared in the doorway. She had heard Janyn's question.

"Nearly so," Kate said. "If you will wait a few minutes, Adela will soon have completed her tasks for the day."

"Come sit in the hall," I said.

Janyn removed his cap, tugged a forelock, and moved to the bench I had pointed out. The structure creaked and groaned. It had not been constructed with Janyn's bulk in mind.

Adela, Kate told me later, had heard Janyn's arrival and gone to her remaining duties with zeal. Kate soon dismissed her for the day and together we stood in Galen House doorway and watched the couple walk toward Mill Street.

"I believe the banns will be read shortly," Kate smiled. "Mayhap I will need to find a new servant if Adela chooses to remove to the castle when they wed and enter Lord Gilbert's employ."

Lord Gilbert had departed Bampton with the mystery of the vanishing holy water yet unresolved. Monday morning at the third hour I sought the castle and told Lord Gilbert of the resolution of the matter.

"Who will be regent," I asked, changing the subject, "now that the realm has a boy king?"

"No one. Many would like the post, and the power, so 'twas decided to avoid the issue. Prince John has the strongest claim, but he is unpopular and knows it. A continuing council is being formed, which will cover the pretense that Richard is competent to govern with the occasional offer of advice."

"Is he?"

"A ten-year-old? Of course not."

"Is this council composed of wise men?"

"Some. But even wise men may have their heads turned when financial advantage is believed possible."

"And the poll tax," I said, "will provide a surfeit of coins to tempt the council. Were you asked to serve on it?"

"Aye. I told Prince John the press of business here at Bampton and at Goodrich precludes regular travel to London."

"He accepted that?"

"Of course. He desires a council he can direct. He views me as too independent for his purposes."

"Is Richard a frivolous child?"

"Nay. He seems sober and well mannered."

"I suppose that is as much as can be hoped for."

"Indeed."

The remainder of the year of our Lord 1377 passed peacefully, as did the whole of the next. No issues troubled Bampton for more than a year, as peace and order reigned in the town. But three days after Candlemas 1379, the frozen corpse of Kendrick Wroe was found in Shill Brook just north of the mill. The lad had perished in the icy water. So men thought.

Afterword

Many readers of the chronicles of Hugh de Singleton have asked about medieval remains in the Bampton area. St. Mary's Church is little changed from the fourteenth century. The May bank holiday is a good time to visit Bampton. The village is a Morris dancing center, and on that day hosts a day-long Morris dancing festival.

Village scenes in the popular television series *Downton Abbey* were filmed on Church View Street in Bampton. The town library became the Downton hospital, and St. Mary's Church appeared in several episodes.

Bampton Castle was, in the fourteenth century, one of the largest castles in England in terms of the area enclosed within the curtain wall. Little remains of the castle, but for the gatehouse and a small part of the curtain wall, which form a part of Ham Court, a farmhouse in private hands. The current owners are doing extensive restoration work, including excavating part of the moat.

Gilbert, Third Baron Talbot, was indeed lord of the manor of Bampton in the late fourteenth century.

Mel Starr